# MAD ABO

Mary Hooper knows more than most people what makes a good story – she's had over six hundred published in teenage and women's magazines, from *J17* to *Woman's Own*, and she tutors evening classes in Creative Writing. In addition, she's the highly regarded author of over fifty titles for young people, including *Best Friends, Worst Luck*, *The Boyfriend Trap*, *The Peculiar Power of Tabitha Brown* and the Spook stories (*Spook Spotting*, *Spooks Ahoy!* and *Spook Summer*) about Amy, a girl with an overactive imagination. Mary has two grown-up children, Rowan and Gemma, and lives in an old cottage in Hampshire.

Books by the same author

*Best Friends, Worst Luck*
*The Boyfriend Trap*
*Spook Spotting*
*Spooks Ahoy!*
*Spook Summer*
*The Peculiar Power of Tabitha Brown*

# MAD ABOUT THE BOY

MARY HOOPER

First published 1996 by Walker Books Ltd
87 Vauxhall Walk, London SE11 5HJ

This edition published 2001

4 6 8 10 9 7 5 3



This book has been typeset in Sabon

Printed and bound in Great Britain by
Cox & Wyman Ltd, Reading, Berkshire



British Library Cataloguing in Publication Data
a catalogue record for this book is available
from the British Library

ISBN 0-7445-7261-4

# CONTENTS

# *CHAPTER ONE*

I think it was the orange flower in the salad that made me realize something was up with Dad. I mean, you don't go round putting petals in your lettuce without good cause, do you? Nor, come to think of it, do you heave out a great wooden canteen of cutlery for what you'd previously called "a quick bite to eat".

"What's all this then?" I said to Dad, leaning over the bowl and picking up the flower.

"Just a bit of decoration to make it look nice," he said. "And put it down again, Joanna. It'll go all black at the edges."

"Is the greenfly on it supposed to be decoration, too?"

In a flash he was out of the kitchen and hanging over the bowl, his reading glasses perched on the end of his nose, minutely examining the greenery.

"I was joking," I said.

He straightened up and glared at me. "Oh, very funny. Look, lay the table if you want to do something useful."

"Who said I wanted to do something useful?" But I lifted the lid off the canteen of cutlery and surveyed the ranks of knives and forks. "A tree has died to make this box," I said severely. "I hope it's made from properly farmed mahogany."

"Mmm?" he said, and he went back into the kitchen and then all I heard was a lot of swearing and a lot of frantic stirring in a saucepan. I went on wondering. It seemed an awful lot of fuss for one date, one woman...

"Don't get fingerprints on that cutlery!" he suddenly shouted. "Make sure it's shiny."

I made a face at the kitchen doorway. "Pardon *me*," I said. "I didn't realize the royal family were coming."

After a moment he appeared again. He was smiling, so maybe the crisis was over and the lumps had gone.

"I suppose it is a bit like that," he said, and he leered soppily. "Tatia ... she ... well, she is quite important."

I stared at him. "You big lump," I said. "You're going soft in your old age."

He went back into the kitchen while I tried to wipe my fingerprints from the knife blades. They went all smeary.

"You did like her, didn't you?" he called.

"Can't remember her," I said.

He was back at the doorway in a trice. "Can't remember her?" he asked in disbelief. "Can't *remember* her?" It was as if someone from outer space had called for the milk money and I'd forgotten to mention it.

"There have been so many," I said.

I was lying. In the couple of years since Dad had joined the singles club he'd only had about four or five proper dates. He'd gone to the pub a couple of times, a film, the theatre, a concert. I'd graded the women according to the venues. The one who got taken to the concert had to be the most important and upmarket; the one who got the pub date was worth only half a shandy and a packet of pork scratchings.

I'd seen a few more women in passing; he'd had some in for coffee and once there had been a singles party at our house, but we hadn't had anyone home for an actual meal before. And I hadn't seen the canteen of cutlery for years.

I thought back. *Tatia*. Bit of an affected name. It was probably made up and her real name was Doreen. I could remember her, though: short, dark hair and she'd had a big bottom with matching bosom. She'd been wearing green suede trousers.

"Did you take her to the theatre?" I asked. Dad nodded and I thought to myself that she'd been just one point down from the concert one.

Dad tore off a square of clingfilm and fitted it tightly over the salad bowl. "She came in here for a drink first and I introduced you – of course you must remember – it was only a couple of months ago. She asked for a Pernod and we didn't have any."

"Have you got any now?"

"Of course." He looked me up and down. "Are you going to change?"

"What for?"

"Because." He shrugged. "Good impression and all that."

"She's seen me before. She's *been* impressed."

"This is different," he said, and when he turned to go into the kitchen I noticed that the back of his neck had gone red.

Slightly bemused, I finished the knives and forks (*and* spoons and forks, we were having a pudding) and put out the salt and pepper, serving spoons and butter knives. I knew for a fact we weren't having soup to start but I put out the soup spoons anyway. The canteen of cutlery didn't come out that often and I felt I should make it worth its while.

"I'm going over to Dee's house – OK?" I said to Dad.

"OK," he said. "Don't get dirty or anything."

"Dad!" I protested. "I'm not four years old."

"Sorry," he said, "I wasn't thinking. Get back in plenty of time to wash and change."

"I'll be here in time to hand out the peanuts."

"Cashews," I heard him say as I was going out the front door.

*Cashew nuts!* I thought as I crossed the road to Dee. No expense spared.

Dee, short for Deanne, has lived up the road from me for four years. She moved from Leicester just before we started at Malvern Edge School and we get on OK. We like the same music and the same boys. (Malvern Edge is an all girls' school, so liking is about as far as it goes.) Dee's a laugh and we have this on-going thing that she's a great bluff Northerner and I'm a soft-in-the-head namby Southerner. We have some good goes at each other about it. I know that Leicester is in the Midlands and not in the North, but I pretend it's North. It's North from *here*.

Dee has a small brother called Fred (I quite often mention the bluff Northernness of this name to her) and a mum and dad. This is two more relations than I've got, but I don't envy her having them. Her mum's one of those women who never stop talking; and talking about things you couldn't care less about, like the amount of time it takes her to do the ironing. Fred is revolting. Think of a nylon football kit with scabby legs sticking out of it and you've got him.

Dee opened the door and we went up to her room, which is in the front of the house, but very small. Fred had to have the bigger room because it was the only one which would house his table-top football game with full team of magnetic players.

"What's up?" she said. "I thought you were coming over earlier."

"I was helping Dad," I said. "He's got a *woman* coming to dinner."

She made a noise which is impossible to write down. A sort of high-pitched *Get him* noise. "Have you seen her before? What's she like?"

"Can hardly remember." I sat down on the end of Dee's bed. "It's the full works, though. Canteen of cutlery, flowers in the salad..."

"Flowers in the salad!" she said. "That's a bit poncey."

"I've seen it in magazines." I shot a sideways look at her. "'Course, you wouldn't know about it – not with your background. You don't often see a black pudding with a flower on the top."

For once she didn't carry it on. "Here, do you think he's quite keen, then?" she asked.

I shrugged. "I don't know."

"Has he told you to disappear after dinner

and leave them alone?"

I shook my head. "He's never done anything like that. I'd *die.*"

"There's always a first time," she said.

We started talking about the forthcoming Rock Festival, which was being held on the outskirts of a town a few miles off. It was over the bank holiday; you could camp, they had one of our favourite groups playing and we were *desperate* to go. Whenever we talked, we planned what we'd take, what we'd wear, what we'd do, though our chances of getting there were roughly equal to our chances of being crowned Miss Stunning Natural Beauty overnight.

"If we didn't camp..." Dee said after we'd mentally got our rucksacks packed down to the last woolly sock.

"We're still not going to be allowed," I said gloomily.

She sighed. "What if we stopped talking about it from now on? They might forget when it is and then we could go out on the Saturday – shopping or something – and then phone home and..."

I shook my head. "My dad knows exactly when it is. He'll probably dig a trench round the house to stop me getting out."

We sighed in unison.

"Everyone's going," I said bitterly.

"It's not *fair,*" said Dee. She leaned forward

and started to pick at an old badge which was stuck on her window. Suddenly she stopped.

"There's a boy I've never seen before just come round the corner," she said. "Quick!"

Before I could even turn and kneel up she added, "Oh no, don't bother. He's wearing glasses. He's just some nerdy brainbox."

I was looking by then. I saw a tall boy, about seventeen, quite thin with fair curly hair.

But I stared in amazement. "That's *her* with him," I said. "My dad's ... you know. The Tatia woman who's coming for a meal."

They were just opposite Dee's house and our noses were practically against the glass.

"Did you know she had a son?"

I shook my head. "And Dad doesn't know she's bringing him. I've only laid three places!"

"You'd better go back," said Dee.

I looked at my watch. "She's early. Seven-thirty, Dad said."

We stared at their backs. They reached my house, turned into the gate and just as they did so, he – the boy – turned and looked directly up at Dee's front window, as if he knew we were there. The setting sun caught his glasses and they flashed.

We dropped like stones.

"Did he see us?" I asked breathlessly, my voice muffled by Dee's duvet.

"'Don't know," she said. "Still, doesn't matter if he did – he's only a boffin."

# *CHAPTER TWO*

"I can't think where Joanna is," I heard Dad saying in a slightly harassed voice as I let myself through the back door into the kitchen. "She promised to be back in plenty of time."

"Oh, don't worry, Dodo," *(Dodo!)* I heard a woman reply. "We're miles too early. The car didn't come back from its service and that train only runs every couple of hours, so it was catch that or not get here at all." There was a pause, during which I imagined her looking at the table groaning under the weight of cutlery. "I hope you haven't gone to a lot of trouble," she said.

Before Dad could say something inane in reply, I closed the back door loudly behind me.

When I walked through to the dining-room, all three of them – Dad, her and the boffin – were standing staring at me.

She was wearing a purple silk shirt tucked

into black cord trousers. The trousers were tight and the silk shirt was open, showing a bit of cleavage. She was obviously of the "If you've got it, flaunt it" school. Boffin was wearing black jeans and a collarless shirt. Not exactly the right gear for boffins – but the fact it was wrong just made him seem more of a nerd.

Dad looked at me, taking in my ripped jeans and grubby tee-shirt and saying *Oh, my God, what do you look like?* with a glance.

"Ah, here she is!" he said. "Here's Joanna. You remember Tatia, don't you, love?"

I stared. Here she was, then. The woman who merited a canteen of cutlery and flowers in the salad.

I felt a quiver of resentment: she was on my territory, in my dining room, taking up my space. She was standing next to my dad and she seemed to have an air of ownership about her, as if she was the rightful occupant of the room and I was the interloper.

"You met a month or so back, didn't you?" Dad went on.

"I think so," I said carelessly. "Hi."

She smiled. *The smile on the face of the Tiger*, I thought dramatically.

I turned and looked pointedly at the boffin. If anyone took the trouble to interpret it, my glance said, *Who's this, another freeloader?*

"This is my son, Mark," Tatia said, and the

boffin turned and nodded at me in a bored sort of way. He shoved his hands into his pockets and looked out of the window.

Tatia smiled at Dad. "Sorry, we got our wires crossed a bit. I thought you said to bring Mark along."

"I did! I did!" Dad said anxiously.

Tatia looked down at the table, heavily laden – but for only three. She raised her eyebrows but didn't say anything.

"It was Joanna and I who got our wires crossed," Dad said. "I thought I told her to lay the table for four, but I must have said three by mistake."

This time I raised *my* eyebrows. That was a downright lie; I knew for a fact that Dad had got only three pieces of chicken sitting out there in some sort of sauce stuff. One of us was going to have to go without.

As I moved towards the television, Dad put out his hand. "Just lay another place, please, love."

I lifted the lid of the mahogany box and did as I was told, sighing a bit under my breath. What *was* all this? What was she doing here having all this fuss made of her? And why was *he* with her? Did he usually go on dates with his mum?

"Sit down, Mark," Tatia said. "Do you want any help in the kitchen, Dodo?"

Dad grinned. "You can advise me on these

chicken breasts," he said. "You should be good at those." At the time, I didn't understand his tone of voice and thought that what he'd meant was *she* should be good at anything to do with breasts, because of hers. How utterly gross. When I worked it out later, I went bright red.

The boffin sat down and picked up a newspaper. I finished laying the table. All was quiet in the kitchen but I couldn't bring myself to look through the hatch to see what they were doing, just in case it was snogging or anything unspeakable.

I sat down on a chair next to the window and stared out towards Dee's house. I wished I was over there. I wished I was over there listening to her mum talk about ironing. I even wished I was on the other side of Fred's tabletop football field pushing a little magnetic man about.

I stared out of that window until my eyes went funny. I wasn't going to speak to him first. I didn't want to and I didn't know what to say. He looked so boring, so brainy, so – boffinlike. He didn't look a bit like the boys that Dee and I fancied. Dee and I always went for boys who looked a bit rebellious; boys who were cool.

I was just wondering if I could possibly put on the television to relieve the boredom when Dad called, "Put out the nuts, Joanna!"

He's come up for air, then, I thought. I got the nuts, opened them and spilt some on the floor. I found a bowl, put the rest in and placed it on the coffee table in front of the boffin. He ignored them.

Dad came out from the kitchen and put on some music. I heard a clattering in the kitchen so she was obviously doing something out there. In my kitchen! The fact that I hated cooking didn't have anything to do with it: she was in my kitchen, using my cooking things, with my dad. And I was stuck with someone who'd lost the power of speech.

Cat got your tongue? I felt like saying. It was clearly up to him to speak first. He was the oldest and he was the interloper.

Tatia came out of the kitchen, smiling. I looked to see if she was ruffled, but she'd obviously been very clever and de-ruffled herself before appearing.

She walked across, crunching nuts underfoot. "Oops!" she said, and she bent down and scooped them into her hand. "You two getting on all right?" It was as if we were at nursery school together.

I stared at her blankly. Did I look the sort of girl who'd get on all right with a boffin?

"I've just knocked up an omelette for Mark," she said. "Another crossed wire – your dad had forgotten he was a veggie."

That figures, I thought. I'd been thinking, in

a vague sort of way, of turning veggie myself. But if he was, then I wouldn't.

Tatia took a handful of nuts. A *handful*. Those aren't your cheap peanuts, I felt like saying. But she probably knew that; she was a gold-digger, after Dad for his money.

"Your dad and I went to the pictures last week," she said conversationally, "and I was supposed to cook him a meal after – did he say?"

I shook my head.

She laughed. "As it happened, the film was so gory that neither of us could eat a thing when we got home."

I laughed politely. When I thought about it, I remembered that Dad had gone out to see a film the week before. I'd thought it was with the crowd from the singles club, though – he often went on group things with them. So how many other dates with Tatia had there been that I didn't know about? How long had my father been leading this secret life?

The boffin turned the page of the newspaper without looking up. I felt like poking him, or dancing up and down in front of him in order to get some reaction.

"Do you like to cook, Joanna?" Tatia asked.

I shook my head. "I hate it."

"*Do* you?" she asked in astonishment.

"It's boring," I muttered.

"You wouldn't think that if you got into it," she said and I took a surreptitious look at her and thought that, judging by her size, she'd got into it a bit too much. "It can be very creative. And so useful."

I made a face. "I really don't think it's useful nowadays. A girl doesn't need to be good at cooking and sewing any more, does she? We've moved on a bit since the Stone Age."

"Oh, I don't mean..." she began, and then Dad came out of the kitchen.

"Ready!" he said. "Take your places!"

As he pulled out a chair for her, a different record came on. A rotten sloppy thing that had been in the charts about six months previously.

A smile slid across Dad's face.

Tatia laughed. "You put this on deliberately!" she said, and she held out her arms.

"Our record!" Dad said, and to my absolute disgust and embarrassment, they started dancing round the chairs.

I made a strangled noise. The boffin looked up from the newspaper and then hastily buried himself in it again.

Dad and Tatia didn't dance for long. Just long enough for me to think, yes – there is definitely Something Up. Then we all sat down to eat.

More clues to the Something were given during the meal. First there was a mention of

Jersey, and Tatia never having been there and Dad saying, "We'll see if we can put that right." Next there was talk of Christmas, and it being dreary and long and a bit lonely, and they looked at each other and Dad put his hand over hers and mouthed something that looked suspiciously like, "Not any more".

Clues came thick and fast for the shrewd listener. Even for the listener who wasn't too shrewd. I thought about the boffin's having looked up when they'd been dancing and wondered if he was picking up clues as I was. But all the time we didn't say one word to each other...

# CHAPTER THREE

What the Something was I didn't want to think about too deeply. Perhaps Dad had decided to see a lot more of Tatia – or Tarty, as I'd decided to call her. Perhaps they were going on holiday together. Perhaps Dad had given up the singles club and wasn't going out with anyone else.

Beyond that I didn't want to go. I'd got used to it being just me and Dad and I liked it that way. Well, I say I'd got used to it, but actually I couldn't remember anything else.

It had been me and Dad since I was three. In books, when someone's mother has died or gone away when they were young, they can always remember her coming into their bedroom late at night, dressed for a party and smelling of French perfume.

Not me, though. I can't remember anything. Not a bean. I feel awful about it, but there it is. I've tried and tried but whenever I manage to get some sort of image conjured up, I find out later that I've just remembered a photograph. We've got loads of them: in albums, on top of the television, in drawers all over the place. There's Mum with Dad, Mum in her wedding dress, Mum coming out of the hospital with me in her arms, Mum and Dad with me – a toddler – swinging me over a stream.

I suppose if she'd known she was going to die she'd have made quite sure I remembered her. She'd have had a video made, or left me letters; in a film I saw recently, a dying mum left a letter for each birthday until the children were grown up. She would have done something to impress herself on me, like a seal onto wax. She didn't know she was going to die, though.

I've sometimes thought about what sort of mum I would have if I could select one. At various times of my life, the mum-target has altered, according to what other people's mums were like or what I needed: someone who'd win the mum's race at school, or iron my school shirts , or (not lately) help me make the things on Blue Peter. Sometimes it was just someone who'd know what I wanted for Christmas without having to be given a piece of paper with the exact requirements and *still* getting it wrong.

It wasn't an emotional thing, because Dad is

OK to talk to, just a vague feeling that it would have been all right to have a mum who could run me up something at the last minute to wear to a disco, or take an interest in buying bras.

I don't think I'd ever met an actual, real-life mum who would have fitted the bill. You just didn't come across an off-the-peg job. The women I'd met in the right age category were too fussy, or too naggy, or too soft, or too loud. Anyway, I was used to it being just me and Dad.

He and I got on all right and sometimes, when I met someone's mum who talked a lot about ironing, I was positively thrilled it was just the two of us. Dad said to me once that what you don't know, you don't miss, and I think that's true. More or less.

Anyway, after the quick bite to eat with Boffin and Tarty, I kept a bit of a low profile. I knew Dad was going to want to talk to me, and I wasn't going to give him the chance.

It was right at the end of the school term so I was out at various things at odd times, and managed to keep out of his way for four or five days. When I was home and he was, I made sure Dee was around.

"I think your dad looks different lately," she said when we were walking back from a school barbecue on the last day of term.

"What sort of different?" I said.

"Different – jollier," she said. She glanced at

me. "Must be love, eh?"

"You're kidding," I said. "Not with *her*. Not Tarty."

"Has he seen her again?"

"Dunno," I said. "He was out last night. I didn't ask where."

"My mum says it's only natural," she volunteered. "She said your dad is still quite a young man..." She paused and we both giggled, "...and it's nice that he's got himself a proper girlfriend."

"Girlfriend!" I exploded. The word in connection with my dad seemed all wrong.

"She might be all right when you get to know her," said Dee.

"I don't want to get to know her!" I burst out. "The bits I know already I don't like. She dresses too young – she always looks as if she's bursting out of things. Her name's stupid."

"Is it foreign?"

"She had a Russian grandmother," I muttered.

"It was the son who looked worse," Dee said. "So *square*. Fancy having *him* around."

I thought about the boffinlike, lofty silence he'd maintained. I thought about his glasses. God, what a drag *he'd* be about the place.

"With a bit of luck I might never have to see him again," I said, and shrugged. "I don't know why I had to see him in the first place.

He didn't exactly set the place alight with his sparkling talk."

"What a *drip*," Dee said witheringly. "Champion nerd of the world."

I didn't say anything, because he obviously was. I didn't remind her that when he'd come round the corner and she'd first seen him, she'd just thought: *boy!*

She nudged me. "He's not like Gavin Loader, is he?"

"You're not kidding," I said. Gavin Loader was, right then, Dream Boy number one for both of us.

"I saw him in town and he asked me if I was going to the Festival," said Dee. "He said he'd get me a ticket. He's mad about me."

"You liar," I said mildly.

She giggled. "He *is* going, though. I heard him say that he's got a new tent."

"I know," I said, "he's already invited me to go along. He said he wanted to be with someone a bit sophisticated, not someone who went round in clogs and sackcloth."

"Actually," Dee said calmly, "he told me it would be a change to go out with a real woman – someone with a bit of grit about them instead of someone fluffy who'd scream the house down if they saw a mouse."

"He couldn't have been talking about me," I said. "I *like* mice."

We reached my house, said we'd see each

other later and I went in. Up to a few years ago, I had to go to Mrs Simmons, next door, when I came home from school, but after my twelfth birthday I was allowed to have my own key and come and go as I liked. Dad works for a firm of estate agents so he's out all sorts of funny hours, showing people around houses and things. He's always done this, and I've got used to it.

This time, though, he was home. He was in the dining-room, trying to fit all the knives and forks back into their right spaces in the cutlery canteen (they'd been sitting on the side since Saturday).

I was quite pleased when I saw him doing this. I thought it must mean that the canteen was going back under the bed and Tarty wasn't coming for any more meals.

He said hello and then he said, very irritably, "How do these stupid things get back in here?"

"You're putting them in the wrong places," I said, because he was trying to fit a big knife into the space where a butter knife was supposed to go. "I'll do it." And I pushed him out of the way, took up a handful of knives and started wriggling them in.

"That chicken was overcooked, wasn't it?" he said suddenly.

"What chicken?"

"Saturday's chicken."

I shrugged. "It was all right. It was just ... chicken."

"That's exactly what it shouldn't have been," said Dad. "Not *just* chicken, when I'd been marinading it for hours." He paused. "Tatia's a fantastic cook."

I started on the spoons. "You should have let her do it, then."

"Jo," Dad said. Just like that but chock-full of meaning and with a row of dots after it. *Jo...*

I didn't reply or even look up.

"I've been seeing quite a bit of Tatia lately. She's a great lady."

I thought to myself, Don't you mean great *big* lady?

"We really get on well. She makes me laugh."

*I* usually make you laugh, I thought.

"And we've decided that we want to be together more. Properly."

I finished the spoons and snapped down the lid of the box. "There's a serving spoon missing," I said.

"I think it's always been missing." He cleared his throat. "Jo, what I'm trying to say is..."

I squeezed past him to the door. "Look, it's nothing to do with me, is it? If you want to see more of each other – fine! I don't need to know the details."

"It's more than just see..."

"Do what you like!" I paused for effect. "I am not my father's keeper!"

"Joanna!" He was cross now.

I stopped in the doorway and put on the face he calls my dumb insolence face. "What?"

"Please don't be deliberately obtuse."

"I'm not. I don't know what it means," I said.

"Dense. Thick." He cleared his throat again. "Now look, love. Tatia and I are very fond of each other."

"So?"

"So," and then he added in a rush, "we want to make our lives together."

Make their lives together! I stared at him, shocked. I thought he'd just been working up to tell me they were – a word he used sometimes – *courting*, or going away for a dirty weekend or something.

He gave me a wry smile. "I didn't mean to tell you as bluntly as that. You've been deliberately blocking me, though."

I stared at him. "This is all a bit sudden, isn't it? You've only just met her!"

"We met seven months ago and we've seen quite a lot of each other. And at my age, I think I know what I want."

I stared at him. "But what d'you mean: make your lives together?"

"Well..." He rubbed his palms and knotted

his fingers. "We want to get married."

I felt my bottom lip tremble.

"We get on well, we love each other. Life just seems ... brighter when she's around."

I suddenly felt quite desperate. "But d'you mean you'd go off somewhere with her? Without me? Where would I go?"

"Silly! You wouldn't go anywhere! You'd be with us."

"Here? In this house?"

Dad nodded. "Of course."

I struggled to control my lip. "With him as well? Where's he going?"

"Mark, you mean?" Dad shrugged. "He'd live here as well, of course. We'd all live together."

"That's *awful*!" I shouted. "I don't want them here. It'll be *terrible*!"

And I slammed out of the room and ran upstairs, crying all the way.

# *CHAPTER FOUR*

Dad came into the sitting-room wearing an anxious expression and – I winced – a spotted bow tie. "Are you ready then, love?" he asked.

"'S'pose so," I said.

He looked me up and down, taking in the torn jeans and the baggy, greeny-black tee shirt.

"You don't want an ... er ... jacket or anything over that?"

I shrugged nonchalantly. "Is it cold there, then? Hasn't she got central heating?"

"It's not cold there. I just thought you might..."

I got up. "No, I'm fine," I said, pretending not to know what he was on about. I added bitterly, "Absolutely fine. Don't worry about *me*."

He didn't say anything, just sighed under his breath. He picked up a box of mint chocolates and a bottle of wine from the table in the hall, pushed them at me and we went out to the car.

While he started the car, I worked my fingers under the cellophane wrapping of the chocolates and pushed the cardboard lid down hard, squishing the contents.

Childish? You bet. It was all I could do. I didn't want him to marry her, I didn't like her – but he wasn't going to listen to me, was he? There was just no point in me even opening my mouth.

Since the evening when he'd announced that they wanted to spend their lives together, we'd been frostily polite to each other. The following morning he'd tried to give me the old "it won't make any difference to us ... you'll still be the number one girl in my life" sort of talk, but I wasn't having any. It was all a lie, anyway. How could it not make any difference to us? How *could* he love me just the same when she was around?

What really annoyed me was the fact that he was marrying her now. Why couldn't he have waited a few years, until I'd left home? It would have been all right, then. I wouldn't have minded.

"Will it be a big wedding?" I asked suddenly. "Is she going to wear a long white dress and everything?" *Squish, squish* went my fingers as half a dozen mint cremes met their death. "And I'm not going to be a bridesmaid so don't ask me."

Dad glanced across at me. "Silly – there's not going to be any bridesmaids; it's just going to be a small affair at a register office. And Tatia won't be wearing a long dress. It's a second wedding for both of us, after all."

"What happened to her first husband, then?" I asked.

"Oh – he disappeared ages ago. Walked out."

Ha! Got out while he could, I thought. "Oh?" I said darkly and meaningfully. "And why was that, we ask ourselves?"

"We don't ask ourselves," Dad said, "we know."

"What then?"

"He ran off with one of Tatia's friends."

"How sordid." I sniffed. "And I suppose she's been looking for a new mug ever since."

It was a good job there was no one driving behind us because Dad suddenly slammed on the brakes and stopped with such force that my head rocked.

"Now look here!" he said, and he grabbed my shoulders hard. I thought he was going to shake me. "I'm not going to put up with this childish behaviour any longer!"

I gawped at him. Dad *never* got into a temper with me. He raved on a bit sometimes, roared rules and regulations and shouted if I didn't do my bits around the house, but he never really lost his cool.

So that was another thing she'd done. Another way she'd come between us.

"You're being *very* selfish," he said. "I thought you'd be pleased to have another woman in the house but instead you're being absolutely unreasonable. I never would have thought it of you, Joanna. We've always got on well and you're getting to an age now – you'll be leaving home soon – where I thought you'd have understood that I needed some company. I've given you..."

He hesitated, breathing deeply. I wanted to carry on for him: "... the best years of my life", but I didn't dare. I just stared, horror-struck. This was *her* doing: in the space of just a few months, she'd turned my easygoing dad into a raging tyrant.

His hands fell from my shoulders and he shook his head. The bow tie had gone crooked and he was red in the face. "Sorry," he said after a moment. "You *are* being a selfish little brat but I suppose it's been a bit of a shock to you. It was a shock to me, come to that. When you reach my age you don't reckon on falling in love again."

I looked at him coldly. I didn't want any emotional disclosures, thank you very much. Seeing a grown man acting like someone on an Australian soap was quite bad enough.

"I just want to say to you," he said, "that I hope, I very much hope, that you and I can maintain the sort of relationship we've always had, and that having Tatia and Mark around will enhance that relationship. You and I have rubbed along OK, but two people aren't really a family, are they?"

I made a sort of non-committal noise, pointedly massaging my shoulders where he'd grasped them.

"Four are, though," he went on.

"Depends what four," I muttered.

"It might be difficult for you at first, but I know you and I know Tatia, and I'm sure, when you get to know her, you'll get on just fine."

I said nothing. If he believed that, he'd believe anything.

"Tatia is longing to get to know you better."

Oh, yeah? I thought.

"I'm determined to make this work, Joanna."

"OK," I said, all false and bright. He was determined to make it work, I was determined ... well, I didn't know what I was determined to do. I didn't want him to be unhappy, of course, but then he hadn't been unhappy *before*, had he? Why did he have to have her? Couldn't we just go back to being how we'd been before she came along?

Dad took a deep, calming-down sort of

breath, then looked behind him, indicated, and drove off.

I stared outside at the houses going by, wondering how to act when we got there. Sulky? Rebellious? Falsely charming? And whatever I decided, what good would it do? He was going to marry her, whatever. Unless, I suddenly thought, I was so awful and little brattish that she decided she couldn't take me on and so couldn't marry him. But exactly how little brattish would I have to be? Would I have to swear at her, gobble my food and slop it down my front? Would I have to say straight out: "You great fat slag, you've stolen my dad"?

I went red just thinking about it. I *couldn't*, just couldn't. And suppose it didn't work as I planned, suppose I was so horrible that instead of her turning against me, *Dad* turned against me and they went off together?

In my mind's eye I could see myself standing outside a children's home with my suitcase, a parcel tied up with string and a label round my neck: *Please look after this selfish little brat. Thank you.*

"Here we are!" said Dad, luckily breaking into my thoughts before I could cry. "This is the flats."

I didn't quite know what I was expecting it to be like. I'd hoped the flat was going to be in a dingy house and have squalid furniture: a settee with holes in, greasy carpet tiles and rotten old net curtains. If it was, then I'd know for sure that she was after Dad for his money.

Unfortunately, it wasn't.

It was on the fifth floor of a newish white-painted block. We went up in the lift and Tarty opened the door and led us into a big room with a wide balcony which overlooked the river.

That room! When I went in I wanted to gasp, but I just about stopped myself. It was *beautiful.* There were lots of lighted candles; it was like going into a church. One wall had lots of paintings and photographs and there was another one covered entirely in mirrors: small glittery ones, medium strangely shaped ones and big ones with stained glass surrounds. Everywhere the candles flickered they were reflected in the mirrors. Thc furniture – well, you couldn't really see what the furniture was like because it was all covered in bright silk throws and there were purple and red and deep blue cushions everywhere. The walls were a dark plummy colour and there was lots of gauzy stuff bunched up and hanging across the windows.

I loved it. I'd have died to live in it. It was the most wonderful room I'd ever seen.

"Sensational, eh?" Dad said, seeing my face.

"Very nice," I said stiffly. I hadn't forgiven him for losing his temper with me. Also, until I'd worked it out, I wasn't quite sure how I was going to act; what I was going to be like.

Tarty kissed dad on the lips and I stood back quickly so that she wouldn't try to kiss me. I handed over the wine and chocolates (one last *squish*) and sat down, looking at the floor when I desperately wanted to look around me. It was such a fantastic room, so mystical and romantic and spooky. I wanted to look at everything in it, I wanted to go round picking up things and examining things and going "Oooh", but I just sat there with a tight, polite smile on my face and stared at the carpet.

The room didn't make any difference to how I felt about her, of course: she'd still stolen my dad. OK, I thought, just because she could make a place look great, it didn't mean she was my sort of person. She might have got people in to do it for her – interior designers. Do me the sort of room to appeal to a man, she'd probably said. Prepare me a man trap.

Boffin came in, shook hands with Dad and nodded distantly at me.

I nodded distantly back.

"Can I get you a drink?" he asked, and I pretended to be studying something very interesting on my shoe.

He repeated the question.

"Oh, sorry, I didn't know you were speaking to me," I said, meaning I didn't know he was speaking to me *at all*, seeing as it was the first time he ever had. I asked for a tomato juice with a dash of Worcester sauce.

"Have a glass of wine," Dad said. "I'll let you!"

"No, thanks," I said. The last thing I wanted was for Dad to say patronizingly that he let me have a glass occasionally, then for them all to watch and see if I coughed when I took a sip.

"I've got champagne on ice," Tarty said.

"Naturally," said Dad. He looked at her soppily. "We've got something to celebrate."

*They* might have, I thought as I sipped my tomato juice. *I* certainly hadn't.

"We'll have it with the pudding," Tarty said, and she went into the kitchen. She was wearing a dress of the same dark plummy colour as the walls, very tight fitting around the hips and going out flouncy.

After a few minutes, an alarming number of dishes started to arrive at the dining-table over by the window; all sorts of bowls and plates and covered containers were brought in. Meanwhile, Dad was talking to Boffin about computers and I was taking a crafty look round the room and wondering what ideas I could pinch for my bedroom at home.

We sat down to eat a few minutes later. The dining-table had more candles on, and there were three big candles on a tripod thing on the balcony. Across the river you could see a factory building in the distance, but it was some way off.

The way the table was laid was weird. Whereas Dad always went to great lengths to have everything matching, she seemed to have done the opposite. We all had differently coloured plates, different glasses, different side plates. They were flowery or striped or spotted at random.

What with all the unmatched dishes containing food on the table, the whole effect was like sitting down to eat at a patchwork quilt. I tried not to like it, but I did.

Dad rubbed his hands together. "Cracking!" he said as she lifted off lids. "I'm starving!"

He sounded as if he hadn't eaten for a week, when I knew for a fact that he'd had a bacon sandwich at five o'clock.

"I wasn't sure what Joanna liked," Tarty said, "so I thought I'd do a bit of everything. Mostly it's vegetarian, of course, but there's some crispy chicken wings in case either of you get meat withdrawal symptoms."

We sat down. There was some Chinese food, but also salady things and different breads and cheesy things. I wanted to hold back and eat in a very aloof and withdrawn way, but *I* hadn't had a five o'clock bacon sandwich so I really *was* starving. I found myself greedily stuffing in food as if I couldn't get enough.

I was just easing off and thinking that I

might have got away without Tarty seeing that I was enjoying it when she said, "Glad you've got a good appetite. I like to see that in a girl."

"The food is absolutely delicious," Dad said, his mouth full. "Isn't it, Joanna?"

"Very nice," I said.

"So many tastes and textures," went on Dad. "No wonder you're in demand."

I pricked up my ears. *In demand?* Then I remembered that Tarty ran her own catering business – executive lunches and business receptions and stuff like that.

I made a sound which denoted slight agreement with what Dad had said, an "Mmm" noise, and Tarty must have thought I was interested in the silly old business because she started telling me all about it. Boffin chipped in with the occasional supposed-to-be-witty comment but he didn't actually address any remarks to me. And I certainly didn't say anything to him, only "Pass the cream, please" (except it wasn't cream, it was fromage frais). I got the impression that he thought I was an unwelcome encumbrance – which, in fact, was just what I thought of him.

And that was our second happy family meal.

# *CHAPTER FIVE*

"And then what?" Dee asked a day or so afterwards.

"Then nothing," I said. "He didn't even speak to me."

"Well!" she said. "The arrogant pig. You'd have thought he'd have tried to make you welcome!"

I nodded indignantly. "Great *dork*," I said.

She put down the eyeshadow we'd been trying out and blinked at herself in my bedroom mirror. "Perhaps he doesn't want his mum to get married again."

"*I* don't want his mum to get married again!" I said. I flopped down onto my bed and sighed. "You should have seen the room though, Dee. You'd have *loved* it. It was all ... all glittery and thrilling. I just wanted to sit there staring at everything."

"D'you think she'll do that in this house,

then? She'll probably take over your sitting-room."

"I don't know," I said. I'd been thinking about this and couldn't decide how I felt. I mean, I'd have loved a room like theirs, but if she changed ours she was ... well, *changing* things. And I'd sworn to myself that I wasn't going to let her do that. Not without a fight.

"Where's he going to go – Boffin?" Dee asked. "Sharing a room with you, is he?"

"Oh, ha ha," I said. "He's going in the spare room. I'm supposed to move my stuff out." I pulled a face. "I've already had a go at Dad about it."

Dad and I used the spare bedroom as a study; there was a desk for the computer and shelves for my school books and lots of my old toys and games as well. I'd always done my homework in there.

"He's not going to have much space. And there isn't a wardrobe. Where are his clothes going?"

"Don't know," I said. "Don't care. Ooh, I'm so mad! Fancy having a boy like that living here."

"It's a wonder they haven't asked you to give up your bedroom," Dee said. "Just because he *is* a boy. They usually get the best rooms," she added sourly.

For a happy moment I contemplated the uproar, the fuss, the outrage and fury I'd righteously create if they tried to take my bedroom away from me. Unfortunately, though, they hadn't.

"Up North you sleep twelve to a room anyway, don't you?" I said, and Dee picked up my pillow and squashed it down on top of me.

We started to look through one of the music papers. We'd heard rumours that an American group we liked were coming to the Rock Festival, but we didn't know on which of the three days they'd be playing.

"Once we've found out when it is," I said, "perhaps we can hang around outside. Bet you can still hear pretty well from the road."

Dee shook her head. "They won't let you," she said. "The police and security move you on. I mean, if you were allowed to stand outside and listen, then everyone would do it, wouldn't they? No one would pay."

"I s'pose so," I said.

"And we've still got to *get* there. If only we had someone they'd let us go with," Dee said mournfully. "A cousin or an older brother."

The same thought occurred to both of us at the same time and we gave scornful laughs.

"As if!" I said.

"His idea of a rock festival is probably a Beethoven concert," said Dee.

"Anyway, who'd want to be seen with *him* – it'd be worse than being seen out with your dad!"

"Ruin our image!"

"What's he do, anyway?" Dee asked after a moment. "Boffin, I mean."

"Haven't got the faintest," I said. "It's a bit difficult to find out things when he doesn't speak."

"Bet it's something awful. Bet he's studying to be an accountant."

"Or a computer programmer."

"Or a *teacher*."

Dee put on a nerdy, strangled voice. "I'd like to converse with you today about religion in the eleventh century, an absolutely fascinating subject on which I happen to be an expert."

"That's him!" I shrieked, though actually it wasn't. He spoke in quite an ordinary voice, but it would have spoilt the game to say so.

Days went by. Dee and I made half-hearted attempts to get summer jobs but didn't manage it, so spent our time loafing about, meeting friends, going round the shops or (very occasionally) doing a spot of homework. I don't know what took up the time, actually, but we managed to fill it.

We were landed with Tarty at odd times, and I overheard long phone calls and discussions about things like beds, dinner services and carpets. Dad always tried to talk to me afterwards ("It's about time I had a new bed, don't you think?" or "I've never much liked that rug in the sitting-room, have you?"), and

I just listened and tried to maintain my uninterested air. I tried to stay just on the right side of sulkiness, so that he wouldn't be able to accuse me of being in a mood – although he usually did.

One evening he said, "How does August 21st sound to you?"

The outside of me shrugged, the inside went all shivery. "It sounds just like any other date," I said carelessly.

"It's a Saturday and it's the date Tatia and I want to get married on," Dad said. "The register office is free – we're free. There doesn't seem to be any point in waiting."

I swallowed hard. It was definite now. It wasn't just this year, next year, sometime, never, it was August 21st. "That's up to you, isn't it?" I said. "You can do what you like."

Dad put an arm round my shoulders. "Come on, love. It's not like you to be so cold and nasty."

"It's not like you to get married," I said, quick as a flash.

"Jo. It won't be as bad as you think it'll be. I promise it won't."

"How d'you know?"

"It just won't. Tatia's a lovely person. She's looking forward to having a daughter."

"Bosh!" I exploded. "What a load of rubbish. You'll be telling me next that *he's* looking forward to having a sister!"

"I expect he is," Dad said, sounding slightly less convinced.

"Oh, right. That's why he doesn't speak to me."

"He doesn't speak to you because I don't suppose he knows what to say. He's shy. And he's frightened of getting his head bitten off – you weren't exactly welcoming when they first came round."

"I wasn't welcoming because I don't welcome them," I said neatly, and that was the end of that conversation.

Objects started arriving at the house; pieces of their lives delivered in crates. Every time I saw a sturdy cardboard box standing in the hall I was tempted to look inside. If there was anyone around I'd walk past as if I hadn't seen it, but as soon as I was on my own I'd be down on my knees peering under the flaps or peeling up strips of sticky tape to see what it held. It was never anything terribly interesting but I felt better for the knowing. Once I found a canteen of cutlery, almost the twin of ours. Oh *yes*, I thought, we certainly need that.

A new double bed arrived; one of those old-fashioned ones with brass and iron railings at the top and bottom. The following day Dad's old bed was taken away and that evening, with a lot of muffled laughter, Dad and Tarty worked at putting up the new one. A bit later

I was invited in to admire the finished article. The bed was very high and had a patchwork quilt on it and some patchwork cushions scattered across the top. I liked it but didn't say so, just muttered that I didn't think it looked right in the room. Dad said that was because I was used to seeing his plain, single bed and that this bed was a statement. I wasn't sure what he meant by that (something rude?) so I just raised my eyebrows, looked at him in vague disgust and went out.

A long wooden table arrived and took up residence in our dining-room. It was thick old scrubbed pine with lots of knots and bashes, and if it had come from anywhere else I would have loved it, but because it was hers I suddenly developed an intense attachment for our old table: white, circular and chipped.

"I don't know how you can get rid of everything we've ever owned," I said to Dad as he piled up the table and our white stick-chairs to go to the second-hand shop. "You seem to be trying to deny the past ever existed."

This "trying to deny the past" was a good phrase I'd thought up in bed a few days before and had been waiting for an opportunity to use.

"What?" he said.

"You're getting rid of our past!" I said accusingly. "You're chucking out all my roots – my only links with my mother!"

"Don't be ridiculous," he said. "We didn't have this table and chairs when your mother was alive. Your Auntie Pat gave them to me when she got her new set."

"It's still my roots," I muttered, the wind taken out of my sails. I was really annoyed – I'd used up my best phrase for nothing.

Actually, I was still confused about how I felt about everything. What was it going to be like? What was *I* going to be like? I already knew I couldn't be out-and-out nasty or rude to her face, so what else could I do – except be sulky all the time? And how boring was *that* going to be?

The thing was, although I really, really didn't want Dad to get married, and I hated the thought of having a stepmother, all the things that were leading up to August 21st were new, different, and – compared to real life – exciting. I mean, when your life just consists of school and home, home and school, then anything out of the ordinary seems interesting and exciting, even if it's exciting for the wrong reasons.

One evening Dad and Tarty sat down to write invitations. It was to be a small affair, I was told, but I was allowed to invite Dee. There would be a few selected aunties and uncles, people from the singles club, a couple of Dad's mates from the squash club and some of Tarty's family and friends, about thirty in all. Dad gave me some cash and told me to buy something nice to wear, and I pocketed it, not saying if I would or not.

It was the exact price of a weekend ticket for the Rock Festival.

Dee asked me if they were going on a honeymoon and I said how could they: where was I going to go if they did? The thought of honeymoons and holidays worried me a bit. Dad and I had always gone away together; what was going to happen now?

One evening Tarty came round in a taxi with two huge cardboard boxes, then she and Dad went out – he was taking her round to introduce her to the aunties and uncles. As soon as they'd gone I got the boxes open, but it was all really boring. One just held lots of kitchen equipment: a food processor and whisks, pastry brushes, little cutters and strangely shaped tins. They were things we'd never had in our kitchen before, which made me wonder if we'd had them when Mum was alive and Dad had got rid of them, or if Mum hadn't been a keen cook, or what. I decided that she probably hadn't been a cook; that she'd been too busy doing other, more interesting and important things.

The other box was just as boring: curtains, tea towels, pictures, mirrors, baskets, trays, lamps and records. Also a shoe box containing lots of little silver-framed photographs.

Just as I reached the shoe box, Dee arrived, so we got the photographs out and examined them at great length. They mostly showed him, the boffin, at various stages of boffin-development. We put titles to them, shrieking with laughter. One of him in his baby buggy, holding a teddy, was "Here is Mark showing early signs of his interest in zoology." One with him looking up from a rag book was, "And this is Mark holding his first published essay" and one of him sitting on top of a piano: "Mark after composing his first concerto."

While we were still giggling about them there was a knock on the door. I looked through the spy hole.

It was *him*.

I ran back to Dee, my mouth an anguished, silent scream.

"Boffin alert!" I said, scooping up the little frames and putting them back in the box. "Suppose he heard us? What shall I do?"

Dee – fat help she was – collapsed in giggles. Boffin rang the bell again and I ran back to the door. Could I pretend I wasn't there? Well, I could have done, but it all added to the drama to let him in.

I put on the outside light, opened the door. We blinked at each other. "Yes?" I asked coldly.

He indicated a large leather suitcase. "I just

wanted to drop this off."

"OK," I said. He didn't move and neither did I. "Consider it dropped." I was amazed at my own rudeness.

"I'd better put it upstairs. In my room," he said.

"I'll do it."

"You won't be able to carry it."

I looked at him witheringly. "I'm sure I'll manage." I took a couple of steps forward and picked up the case. At least, I tried to pick it up, but I couldn't get it an inch off the ground.

He lifted it and heaved it over the threshold. "Where am I going?" he asked.

"Top of the stairs. Turn right." The room – his room – was in a right mess. Dad had been telling me to clear it out but I kept finding better things to do.

He heaved his way up the stairs. I heard him open the door and push the case through. I couldn't think what on earth was in it to make it as heavy as that.

He came down again just as Dee emerged from the sitting-room with a sarcastic grin on her face.

"Hi," she said, smirking. "You must be Mark."

He nodded.

"This is Dee," I said, thinking to get some mileage out of the meeting.

"Ah," he said, "the best friend."

Dee went to say something, then suddenly looked as if she couldn't contain herself any longer. I knew she was thinking of the photos. Her cheeks puffed out, she put her hand over her mouth, then just *burst* out giggling. She tried to speak again but had to double up instead.

I tried to say something – anything – but her giggles were infectious and made me start. We clutched each other, both uttering little snorts and screams.

The boffin looked at us in absolute astonishment. He raised his eyebrows, shook his head slowly from side to side. I wanted to stop but I couldn't. The more he shook his head the worse we got.

His astonishment gave way to a look of contempt. "What silly little girls," he said, and then went out, closing the door firmly behind him.

Two seconds later, I straightened up and wanted to kill myself. How could I have done that? How *could* I have acted like a hysterical schoolgirl? I'd wanted to be so cool, aloof, withdrawn. I'd wanted to be an ice maiden, detached and indifferent. And now I'd blown it and just looked like a silly cow.

Dee blew her nose. "Sorry," she said, "I just kept thinking about him in those baby photos."

When she'd gone home, I went into the spare room to look at the suitcase he'd brought.

No luck there, though – he'd locked it.

# *CHAPTER SIX – AUGUST 21st*

*8.00 a.m.*
I can hear Dad in the bathroom, shaving and singing "Oh, What a Beautiful Morning". I put my head under the pillow but it doesn't block his voice so I come out again.

I stare round my bedroom, which is now crammed with things out of the spare room. The computer is on the floor with its printer and there are stuffed toys sitting all over it. Dad promised to put up shelves for everything but what with one thing and another (ie, *her*) he hasn't got round to it. I can't see that he ever will, considering she seems to be taking up every minute of his time. He's obsessed with her, I've decided. She's probably put a spell on him.

Boffin is now officially installed in the spare room. At least, he's not installed in person, but the room is full of boffinalia and he's moving in over the weekend. Tarty isn't here yet either – though she might as well be for the amount of stuff of hers which has spread slowly through the house. She's moving in after the wedding, which is at two o'clock this afternoon.

*8.30 a.m.*

Dad brings me a cup of tea in bed.

I sit up and say, "Thanks," very stiffly and remotely.

"Lovely morning!" he says.

"Yes," I say. "I heard you singing about it."

He sits down on the bed and my insides squidge up. We are about to have a heart-to-heart.

"Our last morning, love!"

I look up at him and raise my eyebrows as much as to say, You hardly have to remind me of *that*.

"We've got along all right all these years, haven't we?"

"Yes," I say, even more stiffly and remotely.

"And now – well, this is just a new phase in both our lives. A fresh beginning, a different way of life for both of us."

I look at him cynically, thinking that he sounds like the morning service on Radio 4.

"I realize that we're all going to have some adjusting to do, but once we're settled, I think we'll get along fine."

I raise my eyebrows again.

He clears his throat and I know something deeply meaningful is coming. "Don't I always say, Jo, that everything comes to he who waits?"

"Yes."

"Well, I waited and along came Tatia."

"Great," I say.

"And now let's get up and out there and have a lovely day!"

I don't say anything, just flop back on the bed in what is meant to be a symbolic gesture.

He goes.

*9.00 a.m.*

Time is passing, soon I'm going to have a step-mother and there is nothing I can do about it. Well, I suppose there is: if I roll off the bed very hard and break my leg then we'll be at the hospital at midday and he won't be able to marry her. Or, I could suddenly have absolutely screaming hysterics and tell him that I can't bear it and if he marries her I'm going to go off the rails: run away, take drugs and become an unmarried mother.

If I do that, though, he'll probably just throw a bucket of cold water at me and tell me not to be so bloody stupid. And then I'll have to go to all the bother of having a baby, to call his bluff.

Maybe I'll just maintain a stony silence from

now on and for ever. But that will just make *me* miserable – and I know I'll never be able to keep it up.

*9.15 a.m.*
I look through my old books to find stories about stepmothers. All I can say is, there are an awful lot of them and they are all wicked. OK, these are fairy stories, but Penny at school told me her stepmother is horrible and she's *now*. Apparently, she's jealous of anything that went on in Penny's dad's life before she met him, so they aren't allowed to go on holiday anywhere they used to go. They had to move house and she (the wicked stepmother) doesn't allow any photographs of Penny and her sister when they were babies – even if their mother doesn't appear in them! She tries to get them into trouble with her dad and goes mad if he ever gives them money for clothes or anything. Penny says that her life is a misery.

*9.45 a.m.*
I have a shower and put on my new suit. Well, it's a dress and waistcoat, actually. It cost about half what Dad gave me and I'm keeping the rest – just in case there's a way of getting to the Rock Festival.

As I shower I think about buying a sturdy dressing gown. I won't be able to flit from the bathroom to my bedroom and back in my knickers any more. Not with Strangers in the house.

*10.00 a.m.*
Downstairs, Dad tries to make me eat a poached egg but I say I'm not hungry. He eats his two and then eats mine. *The condemned man ate a hearty meal*, I think to myself.

*10.30 a.m.*
A van pulls up and a delivery man comes in with two great big covered metal trays. The van has "Concept Catering" written on the side, which is Tarty's company. Everyone is coming back here after the ceremony.

I go into the dining-room to investigate the trays. There are lots of little bits of things on round biscuits, stuffed eggs, tomatoes with stuff inside, prawns on sticks and twirly fish things.

All made with her fat hands.

*11.00 a.m.*
Dee's mum arrives on the doorstep.

"Is it all happening in here? Expect you're having an exciting morning!" she says.

I smile politely.

"Is your dad in?" she asks, peering round the door. She holds up a present so I have to let her in.

"Oh, lots of changes here already!" she

says, following me into the kitchen. "Your dad's marrying a chef, by the look of all this lot!" Her voice goes all confidential and matey. "I really didn't know what to buy – it's difficult with a second marriage because they've already got everything, haven't they? – so I've bought something decorative. A bit frivolous. What have you bought them?"

"Nothing, yet," I say. It has never occurred to me that *I* should give anything.

"Deanne will be over shortly," she goes on. "She's just waiting for me to press her dress. She said she'd do it herself but the last time I let anyone use the iron they left it standing too long and burnt a hole through the cover on the board."

Just as I am wondering what to say to this, Dad comes in. He sees Dee's mum and shoots me a look of appeal, but I leave him to it.

*11.25a.m.*

She's only just gone. Dad said she wouldn't stop talking.

The present is *awful.* A monstrous vase with gold-painted dragons on it. I want to agree with Dad that it's the most hideous thing anyone has ever seen, but I'm not into agreeing with him at the moment, so I say that it's the thought that counts. He says he doesn't wish to be thought of if it means getting vases like that.

*12.00 midday*
Dee arrives, newly pressed, and then Dad's friend Tony. Tony's driving us to the register office.

Dee looks round the sitting-room and her face screws up in horror. "What's *that* awful thing?"

"Your mum's wedding present," I say.

She groans. "Bad taste or what!"

"That's the sort of thing you like up North," I say.

*12.30 p.m.*
Tony opens a bottle of champagne and we have a toast. "She's a great girl!" Tony says, "Be lucky, old man!"

I sip the champagne and it tastes like vinegar. I'd like to pretend this is because everything tastes sour to me now, since *her*, but to me it always tastes like this.

I try and be stony and frozen but Dee makes me laugh. Instead I pretend it's not happening. We're here to celebrate something else.

*1.30 p.m.*
We leave home. As we close the door of the house, Dad turns to me, looks at me searchingly and then gives me a big hug. I push my nose into his shoulder and feel my face screwing up. I want to cry and cry.

But I don't. I just give a trembly sniff as we

get in the car. Dee nudges me hard, says, "Don't be a soppy Southerner," and that stops me.

*1.50 p.m.*

We stand outside the town hall and lots of people come up to Dad and clap him on the back. Someone from the squash club says, "Not too late to run, mate!" and he just laughs and says, "Not on your life!"

There are some aunties and uncles here, including Auntie Pat, who's Mum's sister. I decide that I *must* have a long chat with her later. Actually, I'm not going to call them aunties and uncles any longer. "Auntie" and "Uncle" is completely uncool. I'm just going to call them by their names.

*High Noon – actually 2.00 p.m.*

Tarty turns up with Boffin. She's wearing a white suit (*white* – who's she kidding?) and carrying pink and white roses. She has a large pink cartwheel hat and because she's short the general effect is of a stumpy mushroom.

"Oh, my God," I say, nudging Dee. "Look at the state of her."

Dee says, "She doesn't look too bad."

I glare at her. *Traitor.*

Boffin nods at me. I nod back. I have to go in the front row with him. There are no hymns or anything, it's all very low key and everyday.

There are no dramatic bits or emotional bits or bits where someone can shout out and stop the wedding.

I stare at the back of Tarty, at her overlarge bottom, and think: this woman is going to be my stepmother. I feel cold.

*2.15 p.m.*

It's done.

We're outside and everyone is taking photos. They all seem to want one of the four of us: me, Dad, her and Boffin. First I have to stand on the end next to Dad, then between her and Dad, then in front of them with Boffin. I'd like to scowl and look bad-tempered, but I don't like the thought of everyone having a photo of me looking ugly. Someone interesting might see it.

*2.45 p.m.*

Everyone else is getting in cars but Boffin has got a flash-looking camera from somewhere and has started taking photos. He poses Dad and Tarty under a dead tree at the front of the town hall, then takes several through an archway, then several more of just the backs of them, walking down between two hedges.

"Arty farty," I whisper to Dee.

I hang about, waiting to be asked to be in some, but he doesn't ask.

"Fancy him not having you in any," Dee says.

"As if I'd want to be!" I snap.

*3.30 p.m.*
We are back in our house and Tarty is acting as if she owns it. She is fiddling about in the kitchen as if she belongs there. Both canteens of cutlery are out. Boffin is still taking photographs.

*3.45 p.m.*
Dad says, would I help Boffin with the drinks? I am just about to move in on Auntie Pat (no – *Pat*) and start my heart-to-heart with her, so I sigh a bit.

I go round with drinks, mostly champagne but cups of tea for some of the oldies. I keep hearing people say, "Smashing couple!" and "Doesn't he look happy!" but not one person asks me how *I* feel. As I play happy hostess I begin to feel all bitter and resentful. *More* bitter and resentful. I wish someone would say something to show they understand. It's not *everyone's* most wonderful day of their lives.

*4.15 p.m.*
Everyone is tucking into the little things that were in the food trays. Everyone is saying how marvellous they are, they've never tasted anything so delicious in their lives, and other lies. Tarty and Dad are holding hands (Boffin took

a photo of just their hands) and are going round chatting to everyone.

There is a wedding cake. Well, they say it's a wedding cake, but it looks like loads of little puff ball chocolate eclairs to me, piled into a pyramid. There is much laughter and jollity as Dad and Tarty spoon it out and distribute it round. More plates are used. Who is going to do all the washing up, I ask myself?

*5.00 p.m.*

At last, I sit down quietly to speak to Pat.

"You look lovely!" she says to me mistily. "My lovely girl."

"Auntie Pat," I begin in a conspiratorial tone (it would take too long to explain to her that I think the word Auntie is uncool). "Auntie Pat, what do you really think of her?"

"Who, my sweetheart?"

"Her. Tatia," I say in a low voice.

Her eyes cloud over and I think I am going to hear something good; something devious and catty, but it seems she's just trying to work out who I'm talking about.

"The woman that Dad's married!" I hiss.

"Ah. Her. Lovely woman," she says. "Delish ... delish food. Bescht food in the world."

I look at her suspiciously.

"And you're a lovely girl," she says to me. "My sister would have ... would have been so proud of you..." To my horror she starts crying. "So proud ... so very proud," she sobs.

I back away.

And bump into Boffin. "Is that your auntie?" he asks, grinning.

I nod. I hope people don't think *I* started her off crying.

"I think she's had a few too many glasses of champagne," he says.

"I think you're right," I say.

"I'll make her a black coffee." He goes into the kitchen.

These are the first proper words he's ever spoken to me.

*6.00 p.m.*

Pat has gone for a lie-down upstairs.

I'm getting bored with them all now. Dee and I go upstairs to play tapes but Dad gets me down again. Dee gets stuck with ex-uncle Jim, who tells her about his days with a rock and roll band.

Out of sheer boredom, I go into the kitchen. I discover the answer to the question *Who is going to do all the washing up?* It is me.

*6.30 p.m.*

Dee makes an excuse, says thank you for having me and leaves. I take her to the door and say that I wish I could leave too – "But I've got Tarty and Boffin *for ever.*"

She purses up her mouth. "He was really rude," she says. "I said something to him and he just looked at me and said really sarcastically, 'You've got over the giggles, then?'"

"Typical!" I say.

"Train-spotter!" says Dee.

*7.00 p.m.*

People are going. There's a big scrum in the hall as everyone tries to find their jackets and bags.

Boffin is speaking to a man near the door (one of their lot) and I hear the man say, "Good luck, then. I hope you get the news you want."

My ears go on red alert. What news is this?

"You're going into an area where there's a lot of competition," the man continues, "but you've obviously got flair."

"I don't know about that," Boffin says.

"Well, let us know what happens," the man says.

He leaves. I'm dying to ask Boffin what they've been talking about but I maintain a cool and distant air.

"I suppose we'd better start clearing up," Boffin says, and I think *Huh*, some of us have been doing it already. This is a new role for myself: *Cinderella*. Cinderella and the Ugly Brother.

*8.10 p.m.*
They've gone. All of them. I'm lying on my bed scowling.

Dad and Tarty have gone out for a meal. They said they wanted me to come, they kept on and on, but I said I'd rather leave them to it. I don't want to play gooseberry; I know I'd only be in the way. Besides, I've seen enough of them for one day.

Boffin has gone back to the flat. I wonder what it is he's going to do? You can't have a flair for accountancy, can you?

I decide to go over to Dee's, but just as I'm sorting out some tapes to take with me, I hear someone stumbling around outside my bedroom. It is ex-Auntie Pat. With a hangover. Everyone's gone home and forgotten about her and it's me who has to sort her out, call a cab and everything.

By the time I've finished doing this it's too late to go over to Dee's so I go to bed.

# *CHAPTER SEVEN*

The following morning I stayed in bed for ages and ages. I usually stay in bed late at weekends, but this time I was *extra* late. I usually make tea on Sunday mornings, too, but I'd already decided that I wouldn't do that any more. If I went in that bedroom and she was in bed with Dad I wouldn't know where to put myself.

About ten o'clock, outside on the landing, I heard Dad, and then her, going in and out of the bathroom, chatting and laughing. I wondered to myself what sort of a dressing gown she had: something in red see-through nylon, perhaps, with black lace. And she wouldn't call it a dressing gown, she'd call it a negligee.

When it went quiet for a bit, I rushed out to the loo and then back to bed. They'd gone downstairs by then but no one brought me up a cup of tea. I wasn't sure if I felt aggravated by or relieved by this.

Just before eleven, Dad shouted upstairs, "Breakfast, Joanna!" and I shouted back that I wasn't hungry. I wasn't used to breakfast on Sundays; we didn't usually get up in time. This was obviously a new regime she'd started.

I was getting a bit bored by then, but I didn't know what my next move should be. I'd have to go downstairs at some point, obviously, and when I did I'd have to sit there and look at them, and eat with them, and (probably, if Dad made me) help wash up and all that. Those normal sorts of things that usually happened without you thinking about them, but which had now become difficult.

I knew I could run downstairs, whiz through the kitchen shouting "Hello and goodbye!" and go straight to Dee's house, but I'd have to come back *some* time. Besides, I was hungry and Dee's mum was a terrible cook.

I knelt up on my bed to look at my notice board. A couple of days before, I'd got some photographs of Mum out of the drawer downstairs and pinned them there. I stared: there she was, in colour, doing all sorts of ordinary and mumish things. She *seemed* real enough – so why couldn't I remember her? Was it because it was too painful to recall and I'd somehow blocked her out? I knew people *could* remember things from when they were babies; Dee once told me that when she was eighteen months old and sitting outside her house in her pushchair, she'd stuck her new mittens down a drain. She said she could remember everyone standing around and shouting at her.

The day that I'd unearthed the photos of Mum I'd also cleaned, very thoroughly with rags and silver polish, the photo frames that stood on top of the TV. There were two big photos: one was of Mum and Dad on their wedding day and the other was of her holding me as a baby. I'd buffed the silver to a shine and replaced them in a central position. They were a challenge; a dare. God help Tarty if she touched them.

At half past eleven I heard Boffin come in and everyone talking downstairs. (Had he got his own key? Was he just going to come in and out as he liked?) Boffin dragged something up the stairs, and then Dad came up, and *she* did, and there was a lot of laughter as they tried to get whatever it was through the door of his room.

Whatever it was eventually went in, and then they did, and their voices went muffled. I leapt out of bed and pressed my ear to the door, straining to hear what they were talking about. Whatever it was, they kept laughing about it in a most annoying way, and *she* had a stupid laugh with a shriek at the end of it.

I heard them come out of the room and leap back into bed. As Dad came by my door he banged on it and said, "Are you ever getting up, Jo?"

I didn't say anything. If I had, I'd have said, Oh, you've remembered I'm here, have you?

Ten minutes later I peered out. I was fed up with being in my bedroom now, but to have a shower I needed to go past Boffin's room. My dressing gown was a stupid pink one that Pat had bought for me; I couldn't possibly be seen in it. And I certainly wasn't appearing in my tee shirt and knickers.

I had my winter overcoat upstairs – it was a heavy old black thing that I'd bought on a market stall. I put this on over the dressing gown and did it up tightly, right up to the neck.

Slowly, quietly, I opened my door and tiptoed towards the bathroom – and of course, just as I reached Boffin's door it opened and he came out.

He looked at me and grinned. "You cold or something?" I gave what I hoped was a withering look and stepped past him. When I got into the bathroom and looked at myself in the mirror I'd gone beetroot.

I showered slowly, looking around the room for evidence of new occupation. A small wickerwork stand had appeared next to the wash basin, containing all sorts of body lotions and hand creams, foam baths, oils and expensive-looking face creams. I guessed she needed a lot of those to keep herself from disintegrating.

When I came out of the bathroom, the overcoat not quite so tightly buttoned this time, Boffin wasn't there.

I got dressed and went downstairs, starving, and made for the biscuit barrel.

"Hi, Joanna!" Tarty called through the dining-room hatch. She and Dad were sitting at the table, reading the Sunday papers.

"There you are!" said Dad.

I grunted something and took a handful of biscuits.

"There's some kedgeree in the big frying pan," she said. "It's still warm."

"No thanks," I said.

"That's haddock and rice," Dad put in.

"I know!"

"It's delicious."

You eat it, then, I felt like saying. I began to munch on a biscuit.

"Want the Review section?" Dad asked, rustling the papers.

"No, I'm just going over Dee's."

"We thought we'd go out for a meal tonight," Dad said.

"OK. Fine," I said. *Well!* I thought, they

were going off and leaving me *again*!

"All four of us," said Dad.

"Celebration," she added, and when I glanced through the hatch they were looking at each other and Dad had got his hand over hers.

"I don't know what I'm doing yet..." I began.

"I do," Dad said. "You're coming with us. I've got a table booked at the Highwayman."

"Haven't got much choice then, have I?"

"Not really!" he said jovially.

She smiled a sort of patronizing smile. "Have you ever been there, Joanna?"

I shook my head, looking at her. First thing in the morning and she had all her make up on: eyeliner, blusher, the lot.

"Nor have I. It's supposed to be super, though."

I nodded. "Can Dee come?"

"Does she always have to..." Dad began, and then I saw a slight movement as Tarty nudged his hand. "Oh, if you like," he said after a moment.

"Cheers," I said, and I went over to tell Dee.

Dee and I sat in my bedroom wearing the outfits we'd worn to the wedding. The Highwayman was dead posh, neither of us had been there before, but we'd heard about it from someone at school.

"Now," I said, "will you be all right using knives and forks?"

"A knife is a sharp thing and a fork has pointy bits on it, right?"

I nodded. "And you use them instead of stuffing the food in with your fingers."

"I'll do my best," she said, and we got up to go downstairs.

She went back for her bag so I got to the foot of the stairs before her. Boffin was just going into the sitting-room.

"Oh, I wanted a quick word," he said.

I looked up at him in alarm. When people say that – teachers and so on – it usually means you've done something wrong. Had he heard us giggling about him? Had he heard what we called him?

"It's OK, you don't have to look like that, it's..." and then we heard Dee clattering down the stairs. "I'll tell you later," he said, and we all went into the sitting-room.

Tarty was draped all over Dad, practically sitting on his lap.

"Good and hungry, Dee?" Dad asked.

"I could eat a horse," said Dee, and then she looked at me and grinned. "That's what we do, up North."

Everyone looked bemused and Dee nudged me hard so that I started giggling.

"We'll never get any sense out of them now," Dad said, and Boffin shook his head slightly, as if he didn't know what to make of us.

Dad drove us to the restaurant. Tarty sat in the front passenger seat, of course, and I thought to myself that not only had she taken my place in the home, but also my place in the car. From now on, it was the back seat for me. Kind of symbolic, that.

In the back, Dee deliberately took up more room than she needed so that I was embarrassingly squashed against Boffin. I could feel him in a line all the way down from my shoulder to the top of my knee.

It took about twenty minutes to drive there.

"It was cosy in the back, wasn't it?" Dee whispered as we got out.

I frowned at her. "You did that deliberately, you pig!"

The restaurant was great: all pink tablecloths and flowers and pictures, and the food was good, too. It was just the company that was dodgy. I felt out of it because Dad, Tarty and Boffin all talked together, and I was left to chat to Dee.

The two of us always had lots to talk about, but I found myself wanting to listen to *them,* in case what they were saying concerned me in any way. And then it occurred to me that *they* were getting closer all the time, chatting and laughing and getting on, while I was getting further away. And then came another thought:

losing Dad to her was one thing, but losing him to Boffin was something else. Suppose Dad ended up preferring Boffin to me? What would happen to me then?

Dee kicked me under the table. "I'm going to the loo. Coming?"

I shook my head, thinking to myself that of course he'd be *bound* to prefer Boffin. Men always wanted sons and I bet Dad had always wanted someone to kick a ball around with and to go to rugby matches with and talk about computers and cars with. *She'd* do all the wonderful cooking and home-making and share the patchwork bed with him and Boffin would be there for manly chat and sporting activities. I was totally redundant.

No one wanted me. I took a deep, trembling breath of self-pity. No one loved me. I felt tears prickling behind my eyes.

"What's up?" Boffin said.

I shook my head wordlessly; I didn't even look at him.

He was sitting opposite, next to Dad, and I think that he moved slightly to block Dad's view of me.

"Come on," he said. "This is supposed to be a celebration."

I had a big lump in my throat; my nose was going runny.

"Are we *that* awful?" Boffin said and I looked up at him and – oh, I don't know, he just looked so puzzled and concerned that a most surprising thought came to me. The surprising thought was this: *Maybe he's not such a dork after all.*

When Dee came back she waited until everyone was speaking and then she whispered, "What were you talking to Boffin about?"

"Nothing," I said. "I haven't said a word to him."

"Only when I came out of the loo you were looking at him in a funny way."

I snorted. "Don't be ridiculous!" I said.

We ordered our puds and I stopped worrying about whether Dad would prefer Boffin to me and worried instead whether I should have ice-cream or cream on my chocolate fudge cake.

All of us (all together) were talking about a photo that had been in the paper that morning when Tarty said, "Well, Mark, when you get on that paper you can do it differently."

"I wouldn't want to get on *that* paper," Boffin said.

"Have you heard about Mark's course?" Dad said to me.

I shook my head.

"I don't know that I've got on it yet," said Boffin.

"Oh, you will!" Tarty said. She turned to me. "It's a photographic course and Mark's had to submit a portfolio with forty pieces of work."

"Oh," I said. I'd known he was at college and trying to get in somewhere else, but I hadn't bothered to find out what he was doing. So, he wasn't going to be an accountant, then, or a teacher, but a *photographer*. Surprise, surprise...

Our puds arrived and we started on them.

"As soon as he could walk he was staggering around with a camera in his hand," Tarty said fondly.

Boffin nodded. "I know I drive people mad – I'm always taking photos."

"He does work for the local paper already," Dad said, trying to interest me.

"So you said." I'd already been told this, but naturally presumed he just made the tea or dusted the office.

"They give him the occasional assignment," Dad went on.

I was just going to ask *what* sort of assignment, when Tarty added, "He's been asked to go to that Rock Festival."

Out of the corner of my eye I saw Dee's spoon, piled with chocolate fudge, stop on its way to her mouth. Both of us stared at Boffin and kicked each other under the table.

"*The* Rock Festival?" I asked.

"The one next weekend?" said Dee.

"Really!" I squealed. Talk about being

surprised; I was *zonked*.

Boffin nodded. "I was there last year."

Dee and I looked at each other. "Can we come with you?" we both said together, and everyone laughed.

They thought we were joking.

# *CHAPTER EIGHT*

"The thing is," Dee said the next day, "we've got to be nice to Boffin. Chat to him. Pretend to be interested in what he's doing."

"We *are* interested in what he's doing," I pointed out.

"Yes, but ... you know what I mean." She looked up at the posters on my wall. "I think I'm going to develop a sudden interest in photography."

"So am I," I said immediately. "You know those two huge suitcases in his room? Well, I saw them open this morning and they contain all sorts of gear for developing photographs. He told me he'd had a makeshift darkroom when they were at the flat."

"Is that right?" said Dee. She thought for a bit. "Maybe I'll think about joining a photography class."

"Really?"

"No, not *really*, just think about it. I'm going to ask him which is the best one."

"That'll be a bit obvious."

"Not to him it won't. He'll be thick about things like that – these brainy types can never suss what's going on under their noses, can they?"

I shook my head slowly, thoughtfully.

Dee looked at me severely. "*You've* got to be nice to him, too. This is our big chance to get to that Festival."

"OK," I said.

"Your dad is bound to let us go; he'll be *thrilled* you want to go with him. Boffin. And my mum will give in, no trouble."

I nodded again.

She looked at me. "What's up?"

I shrugged. I wasn't sure.

"I know it's a drag – having to be all sweet and chatty – but you can go back to normal straight after the Festival."

"I wasn't thinking about that," I said.

"What, then?"

"Well," I said, not quite knowing how to put it. "It's just ... *is* he so awful? I mean, I know he doesn't look much like the boys we like but when you talk to him he—"

Dee gave a scream. "*Is he so awful?* What's the matter with your taste, girl!"

"I just—"

"Is he so awful? You mean, compared to

Frankenstein's monster?" She looked at me incredulously. "You're kidding, right?"

"Right," I said.

What we called the Be Boffin's Buddy campaign began in earnest. The Festival was the following bank holiday weekend so we didn't have long. Dee got stuck in straight away, beaming at Boffin whenever she saw him and engaging him in conversation on the stairs. She even got a book on black and white photography out of the library and asked Boffin how he rated the work of someone-or-other.

It was more difficult for me; I wasn't sure how to act. I found myself in the funny position of having a different personality according to who I was with at the time. With Dad, I was still being hurt and stand-offish, with Tarty I was trying to be unwelcoming and withdrawn and with Boffin – well, Boffin was the most difficult of all. First he'd just been lumped in with the general Tarty package and it was all straightforward: I hated them both and didn't want them in the house. Gradually, though – I mean, possibly my eyes were going or I was suffering from a terminal decline in street cred – he'd begun to improve and didn't seem half as bad as he had done at first.

And now, especially since the meal when I'd had the Very Surprising Thought, I was in a muddle. The withdrawn, unwelcoming bit of me was struggling under the feeling that we were both in this thing – this lumping together of families thing – together; and plonked on top of them both was an overlay of pretend-to-be-nice. Only I didn't have to pretend.

A couple of days into the campaign I was up late, as usual. I'd taken to staying upstairs in the mornings, leaving the kitchen to Tarty and whatever executive lunch she was doing that day. She was usually gone by eleven, so after that I had the place to myself.

I was sitting at the dining table slowly chewing my way through a bowl of muesli (Tarty made her own and it had half a ton more nuts in it than the sort you buy) when Boffin came in.

"I fancy a bowl of that," he said, and he went into the kitchen and clattered about a bit. "I'm glad I've got you on your own," he said through the hatch, and – oh, *stupid*! – I immediately went red.

"What have you been doing?" I asked, struggling to make normal conversation. "Have you been out taking photos every day?"

"Not really," he said. "I've just been sorting things out at the flat – we've only got it until the end of the month. I've been into the newspaper office a few times, though, and they've given me a couple of assignments – jumble sales and church fêtes, that sort of thing."

He came through and sat opposite me. "What I wanted to say to you was, I thought it'd be nice if Mum and your dad got away for a couple of days."

"What for?"

"For a honeymoon." He grinned. "The thing you have when you get married."

"I know!"

"I think it'd be good for them to get away on their own. They wanted to arrange something but didn't want to leave you."

"What about leaving *you*?"

"I'm a fully functioning adult. Practically. If they did go, could you stay with the best friend?"

"Maybe," I said, thinking sulkily that I didn't *want* Dad to go away. But how could I say that without sounding selfish?

Boffin put down his spoon and looked at me. "Yeah, I know it's hard – taking two new people on board, but look on the bright side: when you swan off in a few years you won't be leaving your old man on his own. That's how I look at it."

But now, suddenly, my mind was leaping ahead and I wasn't really taking in what he was saying. I was thinking, how about them going next weekend – next *Rock Festival* weekend!

Dad would surely let me go with Boffin, and if he was out of the way himself then it would be far easier. With Dad around I'd have to take a week's food supplies, phone in every hour and dress sensibly, but if he was away then I could go wearing a nightie and a straw hat and no one would know or care.

"What about this weekend coming?" I asked suddenly. "Would they like to go away then?"

He looked surprised. "As quickly as that? I thought I'd have to talk you round. They might not be able to get booked up."

"Look," I said, "I'll be really honest with you; the Rock Festival is this weekend and Dee and I are desperate to go to it. Dad won't let us go on our own, but if we went with you..."

He nodded slowly, grinning. "Oh, right!" he said. "I wondered why the two of you were suddenly so matey towards me. And so interested in photographic journalism, as well."

I think I would have gone red again but there was probably still a bit left over from the last time.

"So you want me to nanny you, do you?"

"Not that exactly," I said. "We wouldn't be any trouble. We've got friends who're going and we'd go off with them once we were there. We wouldn't bother you – honest."

He ran his hand through his hair. "Well, I could do, I suppose. What day?"

"Saturday," I said promptly. "We'd buy our

own tickets. And Dad and your mum could go off whenever they liked."

He looked at me half-smiling, half-serious. "Well, OK. But I can't help thinking I've been blackmailed."

"You have!" I said, and I ran into the hall to ring Dee, thinking that Dad's favourite expression about everything coming to he who waits – and she who waits, as well – was quite right.

# CHAPTER NINE

"OK," Dee said. "We dump Boffin as soon as we get inside the gates, right?"

"Right," I said.

"Then we look for Gavin and his crowd and latch onto them. We can arrange to meet up with Boffin somewhere later."

"He might not like that."

"Too bad," Dee said. "We don't want to be *seen* with him, do we?"

"No," I said quickly.

She stared out of her bedroom window. "And the bad news is, it's still raining."

It was Rock Festival Saturday. I'd been delivered to Dee's house the night before by Dad, and he and Dee's mum had then had a long discussion about the Rock Festival and drugs, sex and rock 'n' roll. Dee's mum had started every sentence with, "Well, in the sixties..." while Dad had listened politely, shifting from one foot to the other and rolling his eyes at me when he could.

I was officially resident at Dee's house until Monday night, and Dee's mum was responsible for our comings and goings. Boffin was charged with bringing us home by midnight – if we weren't in by that time we would change into drug-crazed new-age travellers (or so Dee's mum seemed to think).

After getting rid of me the night before, Dad and Tarty had driven to the airport – they were off to Jersey for a long weekend. From Dee's window, I'd watched them go; they were completely wrapped up in each other and hadn't looked up to wave. I was indignant about this, but there was another feeling as well: a kind of relief that Dad was occupied, Dad was OK, Dad was happy. Sometimes, pre-Tarty, when I'd been going out somewhere on my own, I'd looked at him and felt a twinge of guilt, especially if he'd had a rough day or something. I still didn't *like* him going off with Tarty but, like Boffin had said, it stopped me having to worry about him. Funny, that.

"Now, I've made you some sandwiches," Dee's mum said, coming into her bedroom without knocking. "I've double wrapped them in foil so they won't get wet."

"You shouldn't have done that, Mum," Dee said. "There'll be plenty of places to buy food."

"Pot noodles and foreign stuff," her mum said darkly. "On a day like today you'll want something more substantial." She held up two oddly shaped bundles. "There are three rounds of corned beef and three rounds of banana." She pushed them into a canvas holdall. "And I've put in a large carton of orange and some crisps."

Dee looked at me resignedly. "Great," she said. "Thanks."

Her mum left the room and Dee said, "Banana sandwiches! Imagine going to a Rock Festival with banana sandwiches! We'll dump them in the first bin we come to."

I was just going to say something when her mum came back carrying a bright yellow shiny mac. "That rain is in for the rest of the day," she said. "There's this old mac of mine..."

"Mother," Dee said. "I am not going to a Rock Festival in *that*."

"I just thought..."

Dee propelled her backwards out of the room. "Do you want me to be a laughing stock? I'd rather *die* than go anywhere wearing yellow."

She shut the door firmly and leant on it. "You see what having a mother is like? You've got all this to come."

"Tarty wouldn't dare," I said, relieved again that Dad was out of the way.

"Actually," Dee said, "you're in a very good

position at the moment – you could get away with murder. It's your birthday soon; why don't you ask for a really outrageously expensive present?"

"Could do," I said. My birthday was only a week or two off but I hadn't thought about it much. It had crossed my mind not to mention it and then see if Dad remembered on his own. If he didn't I could be deeply and horribly hurt.

We carried on getting ready, changing our minds several times about what to wear. Dee's mum called up the stairs, "You'll be wanting your wellingtons, won't you?" but we ignored her.

Boffin came over at midday. We spotted him leaving my house with his camera and gadget bag over his shoulder, and Dee had a squint at what he was wearing (dark green mountaineering-style cagoule) and said it was train-spotter's gear. I wasn't so sure, myself, but I didn't say anything.

We went down to meet him but Dee's mum got there first. She told him he wasn't to let us get too wet and he just looked at her in amazement. We bundled out of the house and put the parcel of sandwiches into a bin in the main street.

Dee and I were on a high. Even just making our way there was exciting, because the closer you got the more packed the roads became with people straggling towards the site. Some had backpacks, some had guitars, some walked under makeshift tents made of plastic sheets. There were punks and new-agers and has-been hippies and babies and ordinary people and dogs on strings and they all had one thing in common: they were all wet.

We caught a bus, and when we got off we still had about a half a mile to walk to the site. Dee and I were both wearing the same long black overcoats, and by the time we got to the turnstiles you could have squeezed them out. We didn't care, though.

"Have you got a backstage pass?" Dee asked Boffin as we went through.

"I wish. I'm not a newshound for *NME*, just a freelancer for the local rag," he said.

"So you can't get us backstage?"

He shook his head. "Anyway, I don't do bands. I'll be taking shots of people covered in mud or fast asleep in a puddle – that sort of thing."

We sloshed about looking at things, Dee and I fascinated by everything in spite of a soggy knowledge that we were both wearing the wrong gear. I would have killed for wellington boots and arm-wrestled Dee for the yellow plastic raincoat, but neither of us would have dreamed of saying so.

There was a field full of tents, where the cool dudes who were there for the weekend were staying. There was a whole section of mobile canteens and vans selling food and there were stalls where you could buy anything from nose rings and hair braids to plastic ponchos and crystals. There were two vast stages where the groups would appear and there was also a small marquee called the comedy tent into which approximately five million people were packed to get out of the rain.

"Do you want to go off on your own?" Dee asked Boffin after we'd all had a quick look round.

He shook his head. "No, that's OK. I promised to keep my eye on you."

Dee shot me a look of horror. "You can't keep your eye on us all the time until midnight!" she said. "We've got things to do. We've got to be allowed to go off on our own!"

Boffin pulled the hood of his jacket further over his head and looked hard at us both. I think he might have been going to insist that he stay with us, that he'd promised Dad, but he must have seen the alarm in Dee's face, because he didn't. "Suits me," he shrugged. "Touting two giggly girls around all day isn't my idea of fun."

"Good!" Dee said. She clapped her hands gleefully. "Come on, Jo, let's go!"

I hung back a little. "Where shall we meet you?" I asked Boffin.

"Eleven-thirty. By that stall over there." He

pointed to a stall selling leather things near the gate. "Eleven-thirty, no matter how many encores they do – OK? Your dad's paid for a taxi home."

"OK," I said, and Dee dragged me off.

It was *brilliant*. Who cared that we were so wet? Our carefully applied mascara trickled down our cheeks and disappeared, our hair – about which we'd agonized for hours – hung in straggly strands around our faces. We bought plastic ponchos and put them on over the black coats and they steamed up and made us feel as if we were walking around wearing diving suits, but I suppose they were better than nothing.

We wandered around taking everything in. We bought candles, hand-warmers, earrings and friendship bracelets. Most of all we bought food. We just kept right on eating: tacos, curry, pizza, doughnuts, chocolate chip cookies and plastic dishes of chips. We saw some girls from our school and, we were convinced, members of the bands just walking around like ordinary people. Time went amazingly quickly as we went from stage to stage, listening to the music and jumping about, sloshing in the mud.

About seven o'clock there was a lull. We didn't like either of the groups who were on and we couldn't get in the comedy tent. It had stopped raining, but it might as well not have done for all the difference it made. We were knee-deep in mud by then and so wet I knew for a certainty that I wouldn't be dry again for the rest of my life.

We went to buy pancake rolls and, in the queue, met up with some boys we knew who were friends of Gavin. He wasn't with them but we were quite relieved about this; neither of us was looking what you might call scintillating. We joined their little gang – there were five of them – and started roaming about together. Two of them were staying in tent city and we went back to their tent for a while and sat around, very squashed but very cool, telling jokes and laughing about different things. I felt a bit funny doing this, wondering whether it constituted the hanging offence of "going off with anyone" which I'd promised Dad I wouldn't do, but I decided it didn't.

It was when we made our way back to the main stage to hear the top billing band that things started to get a bit dodgy. Somehow, in all the crush and confusion, Dee and I got separated. Most of the time she'd been chatting to a boy called Leigh, and I think she deliberately went off with him, though she said later that she hadn't. I was left with the rest of the gang, and then somehow got stuck on my own with this quite good-looking boy called Matt.

We waited down near the front of the stage

for the band and he was all right at first. I felt quite sophisticated and cool being with him on my own, especially when I saw a girl from school and she gave me a beadily curious "Who's he?" look.

Soon, though, he began to get on my nerves: he kept making dirty jokes that I wasn't sure how to react to, then he started talking about girls who were mad about him, saying how he could have the pick of about twenty of them. Whenever I tried to change the subject by talking about a particular group, or saying how great the Festival was, he would say it was pathetic and not a patch on Glastonbury. After thirty minutes on my own with him I decided he was stupid.

The thing was, I couldn't leave him because I just didn't want to be alone in that crowd. So I stuck it out until the top band came on, and then it didn't much matter anyway. There was no way he could spoil *that*.

The band was utterly, *utterly* brilliant, a million times worth the aggro we'd had to get there. They finished their last encore about eleven-fifteen and then there was a massive stampede to leave. Those who were staying in tent city started making their way there and the rest of us began to pour towards one of the five exits. Everyone was singing, shouting to each other, sliding up and down in the mud and slinging mud balls.

I knew exactly where I had to make for and intended to slip away from Matt as soon as I could, thinking that would be easy enough to do in the crowd. He stuck doggedly to me, though, and I couldn't shake him. In the distance I could see the stall where Dee and I were supposed to meet Boffin, and I decided to take a short cut behind a food tent towards it.

"You coming tomorrow?" Matt said, following close behind me.

"Nope! Couldn't get tickets," I lied. I tried to look ahead and see if Boffin was there waiting.

Just then, Matt caught up with me and grabbed my arm. We were in a little alleyway between the food tent and a fence so it was quite narrow and there were only a few people tramping past. "I'd better have that goodnight kiss now, then," he said.

I knew I ought to have pushed him away, but I was too surprised. I just stood there and stared. And then he lunged.

Now, I haven't got that much experience; I haven't kissed that many millions of boys, but I kissed Pete White at the Valentine's disco and Sam Jaggard at Melissa Swan's party; I've kissed enough to know that this kiss was revolting. Like being snogged by a large, slobbery water mammal. It rated minus ten on the desirability scale.

But I didn't get very long to sample it.

"You ready?" a voice behind me said. Someone put a hand on my shoulder and I turned to see Boffin standing there.

Matt looked as surprised as I was, but without the "Phew, what a relief" factor. Boffin was obviously older than him, and bigger. The two of them stared each other out, then Matt said, "See you, then," and sloshed away.

I was so pleased to see Boffin I felt like doing something *mad* – like flinging my arms round him – but of course I didn't. I just stood there breathing deeply and raggedly. I should have pushed him away, I thought. I shouldn't even have had the quick sample.

"Who was that?" Boffin asked.

"Some nerd."

"You shouldn't get yourself in a position where you're on your own with nerds."

"I know," I said a bit shakily.

Other people had started to come down the alleyway. A tall guy in a plastic cloak ran past us, hooting with laughter.

"It's OK," Boffin said, steadying me. "Nothing would have happened. I spotted you earlier; I was following you."

I looked at him and didn't know what to say. I felt silly, and small, and grateful all at the same time. "Cavalry to the rescue," I said. "Cheers."

"Any time," he said, just like that.

*Any time.* As he looked me in the eyes the

truth suddenly hit me with the force of a grand piano. He was all right; I really liked him. No, more than that: *I fancied him.*

Yes, I, Joanna Pearson, being of sound mind and normal disposition, fancied a boffin.

# CHAPTER TEN

"Look," I said to Dee some days later, "all I'm asking is, why did we call him a boffin?"

She shrugged. "Because he is."

"He's not though, is he?" I said earnestly. "Not really. He doesn't dress like one or talk like one or have boffin hobbies. He isn't an accountant or a computer freak or..."

Her face screwed up. "Why are we talking about him? Who wants to talk about boffins when..."

"He's not a boffin," I said doggedly.

"...when there are hunks to talk about?" she went on. "Leigh asked me skating. Why don't you come? You might see Matt again."

"I don't want to see him again," I said with a shudder. "And if you'd been kissed by a lump of blubber you wouldn't, either."

"Oh, come on," she said. "A kiss is nothing, is it? What did you expect – that he'd kiss you on the hand? Is that what people do down South?"

But I couldn't even joke about it. "He was revolting," I said, "and what was worse – he thought he was wonderful. He really fancied himself."

Dee bounced down onto the bed beside me. "They all do," she said.

Boffin doesn't, I thought. But I didn't say it. Instead I said, "It's just the glasses, isn't it?"

"What is?"

"The reason we called him a boffin. If he hadn't been wearing glasses we wouldn't have called him that."

Dee looked at me in amazement. "I don't know. Does it matter? Call him something else if you want." She closed her eyes. "I'm having this fantasy about skating, and Leigh and I are dancing round the rink all on our own..." She began to hum, swaying backwards and forwards. "That would be dead romantic, wouldn't it? Alone on the rink, in the darkness, just the two of you skating around to a smoochy record."

"You can't skate," I said. "You can't even stand up on the ice."

"I'd learn," she said. "Leigh would teach me."

I stood up and looked out of the window towards my house, wondering where he was, what he was doing. Since the Rock Festival I'd spent a stupid amount of time doing that. "Have you done all your school projects?" I asked Dee.

"Nearly. There's just the one on astrology. Oh, by the way, what do you want for your birthday?"

"I don't mind," I said. "Surprise me."

"What are you getting from your dad?"

"A CD player," I said. "At least, that's what I've asked for."

"You'll get it," she said. "You're bound to. They won't dare not give it to you in case you go on the turn."

"I always am on the turn now. Since *she* came on the scene." But actually, when I thought about it, I wasn't, not really. I still did the occasional tight-lip and withering glance, but it was just too much of a strain to be mean and moody all the time. Especially now. I'd even converted their names back to their real ones. They were Mark and Tatia now, except when I was talking to Dee.

An orange VW Beetle drew into a space on the other side of the road, near my house. As I watched, a girl got out of the driving seat, came round to the passenger side and started wrestling with the door.

It opened after a bit of effort, and to my surprise Boffin got out. He reached behind the seat for his gadget bag, and he and the girl walked up the path of my house together.

I found my voice. "Look!" I croaked. "Mark ... er ... Boffin and a girl!"

Dee sat up straight and looked out. "Who is she?"

"Don't know," I said in a stunned voice.

She had short dark hair that was spiky on top and – from what I could see – looked pretty. Too pretty. She was dressed ethnic – long droopy skirt, patchwork waistcoat and lots of coloured beads.

"I expect it's his girlfriend," Dee said, shrugging.

I peered closer to see if they were holding hands. I couldn't be sure. "He didn't say he'd got one," I said, feeling as if someone had punched me in the stomach.

"Why should he?" said Dee.

We watched them go into my house. He and I had chatted quite a bit over the last few days, since *then*. It hadn't been personal sort of chat, but I was sure he'd have mentioned a girlfriend. Also since then, it was no longer possible for me to be withdrawn and aloof with him – I'd given that up as a bad job. I was trying to be normal, but found it hard to work out what "normal" was. What was the normal way of acting with someone you thought was an interloper and a boffin, but who then turned out to be someone you fancied *and* your stepbrother?

"I expect he's brought her back for a quick

snog," Dee said. "Those cars are draughty."

I stared at her. "D'you think it *is* his girlfriend?"

"Don't know," she said. "So what? Even boffins have them."

I looked at my watch. "I'd better be getting back."

"Spoilsport!" said Dee. "You're going back to stop his fun."

"No, I'm not," I said. "I just ... just told Dad this morning that I'd clear up the mess in the bathroom."

"Since when have you ever bothered about things like that? Do it later."

"I can't," I said abruptly, and there shot into my head a vision of Mark and this girl spread out on our settee, kissing passionately. "I'll see you later."

"Shopping tomorrow – yes?"

"If you like," I said, all distracted.

"I'll pop over about..."

But I never heard exactly when she was going to pop, because I was halfway out of the front door.

*A girlfriend*, I thought as I hurriedly crossed the road. A girlfriend was something I hadn't considered. There had been no hint of one. And wouldn't she have come to the wedding or the celebration meal? But maybe she'd been on holiday... Maybe they were in there now, making up for lost time. What would I say if I opened the front door and they were all over each other in the hall?

"Hello!" I called as I pushed the door open. I held my breath as I waited to hear where the reply would come from. Suppose they were *upstairs*...

"Hi!" came an answering call from the kitchen. I went through, smiling brightly.

"Joanna, this is Sarah," Mark said, and I looked at him and thought how funny it was that once you acknowledge that something is so (ie, admit that you fancy someone) everything changes. Like, I found his gold-rimmed glasses a positive plus now; I found them arty and witty; everyone should have such glasses. Everyone should have short blond hair as well.

The girl and I exchanged a "Hi" and looked each other up and down. God, she really was pretty. I felt sick – and also small and insignificant.

"We're just having coffee," Mark said. "Do you want one?"

"Please!"

While Mark fiddled about grinding beans and filling glass jugs (proper coffee was another thing Tatia had brought into our daily lives), I sat at the dining-room table and listened to what they were talking about, waiting for clues as to who she was.

Mark carried three mugs through and passed me one. We moved into the sitting-room and all sat down and looked at each other. I wasn't going to go anywhere and leave them alone. It was my house, after all. She'd just have to put up with me.

We talked about the Festival; Sarah hadn't been. She'd been to Glastonbury the year before, though, and said that ours wasn't a patch on that one.

"Sarah's in my group at college," Mark said, and I nodded politely. That told me nothing.

"This waiting's the worst bit, isn't it?" Sarah said to him, and they discussed whether or not they'd get in to the college they'd applied to, where Mark was going to do Photography and she was going to do Fashion.

They started talking about people they both knew, laughing about people I'd never heard of. I sat on doggedly, drinking my coffee and looking around. The sitting-room had undergone changes since Tatia had arrived. Coloured blanket things had been thrown over the settee and chairs, and scatter cushions had appeared. A great big rug with suns and moons hung on the back wall, and there were paintings on the other walls. We had ornaments now – candlesticks and chunky baskets with dried flowers in them. The two photographs of Mum still stood on the television, though.

Mark and Sarah moved to talking about the

local paper, a photographic exhibition, a book I hadn't read, and I still sat on.

Tatia came in and, after a while, asked Sarah if she was stopping for supper. Sarah said no. Tatia then called me into the kitchen. I went a bit rebelliously, wondering if she was going to ask me to go upstairs and not play gooseberry.

She didn't. She wanted to ask me about my birthday.

"Your dad knows what you want for a present, but I wondered if you'd like us to throw a party or something," she said.

"I hadn't thought," I said. *A party*. I'd never had one of those. "What sort of party?"

"Not the jelly and ice-cream sort!" she said. "A buffet or something – or whatever you like." She smiled. "I *am* a catering company."

I shook my head slowly. "I don't think so," I said. Parties were dodgy things: you sat around all day worrying that no one would come and then a squillion people gatecrashed and the police had to be called. I looked at her. "Thanks anyway."

My relationship with her had undergone a transformation, too. She didn't know it, but she'd changed from being the interloper, the woman who'd taken my dad away, to being the mother of the boy I fancied.

Another thing: now her name wasn't Tarty any more, she'd stopped being fat and vulgar and seemed quite ordinary. God, I thought, life was *weird.*

"Just a special dinner, then, perhaps. With Dee?"

I thought quickly. If non-family came, then perhaps Sarah would also come.

"No, that's all right," I said. "Just us."

It was a really brilliant birthday meal – three courses and all sorts of interesting bits and pieces. By the end of it I felt totally stuffed.

The four of us flopped in the sitting-room for a while, then Boffin offered to get coffee. Tarty said no, she'd do it.

She was gone a while, during which time I thought to myself that we were certainly eating a lot better since she'd been around. *And* I'd had my presents wrapped with *ribbon on.*

Suddenly, from the kitchen, she called, "Lights!" and Dad jumped up and turned off all the lights in the room. A moment later she appeared round the corner carrying a white-iced birthday cake covered with flickering candles.

I stared, thrilled. I'd never had a proper birthday cake before.

But as I thought that, in my head I suddenly saw, instead of Tarty, a woman wearing a red dress, carrying a cake through that same door. It was a big white cake, just like the one Tarty carried, but it had only three candles.

I stared, not understanding, and then I realized what had happened. I burst into tears and ran upstairs.

A small amount of time went by and then Tatia came up and tapped on my bedroom door.

I opened it a crack and spoke to her, but couldn't tell her what it was that had upset me.

"My cakes don't usually have that effect on people," she joked, and I said no, it had looked lovely, and I'd be down soon; sorry.

After another interval Dad came up and I let him in. He sat down on my typing chair while I snuffled on the bed. He asked me what on earth was the matter and said that I'd upset Tatia.

"I thought you were getting on all right," he went on worriedly. "I suppose I've been allowing myself to get a bit complacent about it but I honestly thought..."

"It's not that," I said. "I'm not upset about her being here or you marrying her or anything. I'm not *that* sort of upset at all."

"What, then?"

"Well," I said carefully. "Can you remember – did my mum have a red dress?"

He looked at me, bewildered. "I don't know. How d'you expect me to remember that?"

"All right then – did I have a birthday party

when I was three? Did I have a proper cake with candles?"

He closed his eyes. "Yes, you did," he said after a moment.

"I *knew* I had," I said. "I've *remembered* her!"

# CHAPTER ELEVEN

It would be nice to be able to say that after that evening, images and memories of Mum came flooding in so that I could suddenly remember lots about her, but they didn't. I felt better, happier, though, knowing just that one thing. Before, it had been difficult to imagine having a mum at all. I mean, I knew I *had* had one, but it had been a bit like believing in fairies – you thought to yourself that yes, it would be nice if it was true, but you really needed a bit of proof.

Now I had the proof.

It didn't affect my relationship with Tatia. I mean, I didn't suddenly fall into her arms sobbing, begging her to please be my new mother – but I *did* feel grateful to her. So much so that the week before we went back to school she came and helped me choose a new duvet cover for my bedroom. This in itself was amazing and revolutionary, and was brought about because (a) I knew she had a good eye for those sorts of things; (b) I liked having someone other than me interested in my duvet cover; and (c) I wanted to keep in with her because she was Mark's mum.

Where he was concerned I'd have liked our relationship to go on rewind. When I thought about how cold I'd been to him, how offish, how silly-cowish and giggly, I could have died. He was friendly enough to me, but I'd have liked *more* than friendly. I didn't know if I'd messed things up for good. Would he always see me as I'd been at first?

I didn't think it was fair. I don't know why, when you meet someone you're going to fancy later, you can't have an early warning system; a little light inside you which goes on and a message which flashes to your brain saying: *Danger! Don't act like a stupid cow!* It would really be a great help.

On the last Friday before going-back-to-school Monday I was fed up. Dee had gone away with her family that week so she hadn't been around to chat to (not that I'd done much in the way of important chatting, because I hadn't worked out how to tell her about the de-boffining of Mark) and everyone else was out.

It was where they were out (OK, where *he* was out) that was making me more fed up.

Sarah had called round for him earlier and they'd gone off in the Beetle. I wasn't sure where they'd gone, but I'd decided that they'd taken a picnic to the seaside, and I could almost *see* them sitting on the rocks, his arm hanging loosely round her neck, dangling their feet in the water and gazing out to the horizon.

About midday I'd changed the scenario slightly: they'd spread a white cloth on the sand and were sharing a delicious Concept Catering lunch, so I was quite surprised when I heard the lawnmower noise of the Beetle's engine outside and then a key in the lock.

I darted into the hall. That was another thing – *darted.* You couldn't do the old playing it cool bit when you were under the same roof – especially if he might think that playing it cool was you just being stand-offish and unfriendly again.

"Sarah not coming in?" I asked, pleased because it was obvious she wasn't.

He shook his head. "She's gone home to get the second post. Apparently our notification letters should definitely arrive today."

"From the college you've applied to?"

He nodded. "We were hanging around at school waiting for them to arrive, then got told they'd gone to our home addresses."

We went into the kitchen. "Is it just you and Sarah wanting to go to that particular place?" I asked.

He shook his head again. "There are four of us, but we won't all get in. Max definitely will – he's submitted the most amazing portfolio of stuff."

"Who's Max?"

"Sarah's boyfriend. It's his Beetle."

"Oh," I said.

"What are you smiling at?"

"Nothing. Coffee?" I got the filter thingies out but he shook his head.

"I'm awash with it. We've been drinking it all morning."

"Will the letter come here?" I asked. "Won't it go to your old address?"

"No, I thought of that. When I filled out the notification envelope I put this one."

There was a sudden noise from the hall and we both jumped and looked at each other, but it was only Tatia coming in.

"Anything?" she asked. She came through to the kitchen looking strangely normal; her bottom smaller than ever. Funny, that.

"Nope," said Mark. "Definitely second post today, though."

"We've heard that before," she said. She started sorting through drawers. "My electric whisk has gone on the blink; I've rushed back for..."

There was another noise from the front door and we all three looked at each other.

Mark peered round the kitchen door into the hall.

"Large brown envelope," he said in a doom-laden voice. "That's it."

We went out and looked down at it on the mat.

"Well, it's not going to bite," Tatia said. Mark didn't go to pick it up so she said, "Do you want Joanna and me to go back into the kitchen while you open it?"

He didn't reply. The only part of him which moved was a muscle twitching in his cheek.

Tatia made a raised-eyebrow face at me. "Come on, then," she said, and we went back in and closed the door.

We pressed our ears to the wood. It seemed *ages* before we heard a movement, a crackle as he picked up the envelope, and then ages more before there was a tearing sound.

We held our breath. Tatia's eyes were shut; I don't think she realized it, but she was holding one of my hands tightly in hers.

Suddenly there was a roar from outside, a shout of "Yeah!" We flung open the door and rushed out.

"Made it!" he shouted. "I'm in!" and he picked up both of us, one in each arm, and tried to swing us round.

Laughing and unsteady, we jiggled around shouting "Hurray!" and "Well done!" and all that, then Tatia broke away saying, "I must get back. I haven't done the puddings yet!"

She went into the kitchen and I heard her churning through the drawers, while Mark, grinning all over his face, made for the phone in the hall. "September 12th!" he was saying. "They don't exactly give you a lot of time."

I sat on the stairs hugging myself, thrilled because he was thrilled. I imagined him coming home every evening with news of exciting assignments, tales of photo sessions with top bands and snippets of gossip about rock stars.

Tatia came out of the kitchen brandishing a whisk.

"Oh, well," she said to me, smiling, "it looks like you'll be able to have your spare room back."

I stared at her.

"Hardly worth getting that bedroom all sorted, was it?"

"What do you mean?"

"Well, he'll be moving to Sheffield, of course," she said. "Yorkshire. A bit of a long way but it's the place he wanted."

"Oh," I said. Not for one moment had I thought about where the course might be. *Sheffield.* It was miles away – at least two million. I felt quite desperate. I felt I might cry.

"I'll really miss him but..." Tatia stopped suddenly and looked at me keenly. "Oh," she said. "I see."

I tried to swallow the big lump in my throat.

She raised her eyebrows. "So you're going to miss him, too."

I nodded, just slightly.

She put out a hand and squeezed mine. "We'll visit," she said. "And the terms are short – he'll keep coming back." She waved the whisk. "I'm off to fatten businessmen. Tell Mark I'll ring later – and tell him he's a star."

I sat on the stairs while he made three or four phone calls.

"Me and Max!" he said when he finally put the receiver down. "Just me and Max!" He leapt in the air and swiped at the light.

"It's terrific. I'm really pleased for you," I said in as happy a voice as I could manage. "Your mum said she'd ring later, and to tell you you're a star."

He suddenly lifted me off the stairs in a bear hug. "Best course in the country," he said. "I'm not only a star, I'm a genius!"

"Of course you are," I said into his shirt, and I hugged him back as hard as I could.

"I'll miss you," he said, and I thought, amazed: Oh, *wow*, did he really say that?

"I'll miss *you*," I said. "I didn't even realize you were going. Not so far..."

He loosened his grip, held me at arm's length and looked at me.

Then he kissed the top of my head.

And that, in spite of my fervent yen for a lip-crushing, swoon-inducing moment of passion, was as far as it went. For the moment.

But I was perfectly happy, because I had a definite feeling that it *might* go further.

Doesn't everything come to she who waits?

## THE BOYFRIEND TRAP
Mary Hooper

Arriving at her older sister's flat, with a bag full of teen mags and a head full of True Love, Terri is dismayed to discover that Sarah doesn't appear to have a single boyfriend! Something must be done – and quickly!

"A brilliant read." *My Guy*

## BEST FRIENDS, WORST LUCK
Mary Hooper

Moving from the city to a new life in the country is not Bev's idea of fun. Who will she find to talk to? What will she find to do? And how on earth will she manage without her best friend Sal?

"Sharp-witted... Great fun." *The Daily Telegraph*

THE PECULIAR POWER
OF TABITHA BROWN
Mary Hooper

*"I looked down at myself. I saw black fur. I saw paws. And I knew immediately what had happened."*

Tabitha Brown is surprised to learn she's been left a cat cushion in Great-aunt Mitzi's will. But soon, the true nature of her aunt's legacy becomes clear. Landing on her feet, Tabitha realizes she has inherited a peculiar and extraordinary power – and she quickly sets about making good use of it!

Intriguing and highly enjoyable, Mary Hooper's story is guaranteed to make you purr.

FREEWHEELERS TO THE RESCUE!
Eric Johns

*"We solemnly swear to seek adventure, excitement and danger and to rescue anyone in peril."*

So proclaim the Freewheelers, Gina, Claire and Mandy, a bicycle gang with bags of enthusiasm and just one thing missing – bicycles. When they discover that a little girl has been kidnapped in their home town – with a £1000 reward for her rescue – it seems like the perfect opportunity to put their code into practice and earn the bike money they need. But things don't go quite as planned, and before they know it, the girls are freewheeling straight into trouble...

